The
Nearest
Far
away
Place

The
Nearest
Far
away
Place

HAYLEY
LONG

HOT
KEY
BOOKS

First published in Great Britain in 2017 by
HOT KEY BOOKS
80–81 Wimpole St, London W1G 9RE
www.hotkeybooks.com

A CIP catalogue record for this book is available from the British Library.

ISBN: 978-1-4714-0626-3
also available as an ebook

1

This book is typeset in Bembo 12/16.5 pt by
Palimpsest Book Production Limited, Falkirk, Stirlingshire
Printed and bound by Clays Ltd, St Ives Plc

Hot Key Books is an imprint of Bonnier Zaffre Ltd,
a Bonnier Publishing company
www.bonnierpublishing.com

*For anyone who has ever loved someone
and lost them.*

'People like us, who believe in physics, know that the distinction between past, present and future is only a stubbornly persistent illusion.'

Albert Einstein

0

Me and my brother Griff grew up living out of suitcases.

We were babies in London, little kids in Munich, still pretty small in Shanghai and getting bigger in Barcelona. By the time we came to live in Brooklyn, we thought we were the coolest British kids on the block. And perhaps we were – there weren't any others.

Along the way, we had friends called Matilda and Maxim and Ibrahim and Li and Emilio and Lester and they were scattered like breadcrumbs in a trail behind us.

We had passports filled with border stamps and Coke cans filled with foreign coins.

We knew lots of words that meant hello and just as many that meant goodbye.

And, best of all, we had parents whose feet never stopped moving. They were teachers. And they taught their way around the world from school to school and city to city and took us with them. And that suited me and Griff just fine.

Then one day, everything changed.

PART ONE

–

Neither Here Nor There

1

The day Griff turned thirteen it was hot.

Really hot.

Hotter than hell probably.

In fact, it was such a scorcher that the whole of New York seemed to be melting into the ground. We were driving back in our hire car from our summer vacation – or should I say holiday – and as we crept closer to Brooklyn, I kept catching glimpses of Manhattan in the distance. Its tall skyscrapers looked wobbly with the heat.

The car radio was on but only very quietly. Sometimes pop songs were playing and sometimes it was just random chat. Mostly I wasn't listening anyway. But then I heard a DJ say, *It sure is hot today, folks.*

Genius, I said. But it was just a word in my head. I didn't actually say it for real. I didn't have the energy.

And for those of you listening in NYC, the temperature is

*now nudging forty degrees! That's four-zero degrees. So stay cool,
people, and stay safe. Keep slapping on that sunblock and slipping
on those sun hats and shades.*

I shuffled my stiff legs and sighed. And then I decided
I couldn't keep quiet any longer. I *had* to moan. Out loud.

But I wasn't fast enough.

'Oh *maaan!*' The groan was from my brother Griff.
'What sort of birthday is this? I'm sweating my fanny off.'

'*Good God, Griff!*' said Mum from the front passenger
seat. 'Just remember you're *British!*'

'Sorry,' muttered Griff, and his face went a bit red. After
a moment of embarrassed silence, he said, 'Can you turn
up the air conditioning?'

'Yeah,' I said. 'Turn it up.'

Mum reached up, slid open the mirror in her sun visor
and looked at us. 'So you're awake then?'

'I've been awake the entire flipping time,' said Griff.

'We *knew* that,' said Dad, cutting in on the conversation.
'We've enjoyed listening to that fantastic tune on your
computer game. It hasn't bugged the bejeezus out of me
at all.'

'It's Temple Run 2,' said Griff. 'And it's not a computer
game. It's an app.' In spite of everything, he suddenly
smiled and waggled his right hand in the air. It had a
brand-new phone stuck to it.

I bit back a grin. It was a big day for my little brother.
His thirteenth birthday and his first decent phone.

Mum said, 'That's lovely, Griff. And I'm glad you're 'appy – but actually I was referring to *him*.' She waved her hand over her shoulder at me.

'I've been awake since Massachusetts,' I said.

Mum looked at me in her make-up mirror. 'Chatty as ever, Dylan.'

I shrugged a hot shoulder. 'There's no point talking just for the sake of it, is there?'

Mum rolled her eyes. 'It doesn't *cost* anything to chat to your family, Dyl. You're not gonna run out of credit.' She shook her head at her mirror and then laughed.

I couldn't think of a decent response. So I laced my fingers together, stretched out my arms and cracked my knuckles. One by one. *Crack. Crack. Crack. Crack.* It's something I've always been good at.

Griff shoved me in the side. 'Stop it,' he said. 'It gives me the shivers when you do that.'

I shoved him back.

'Hey, cut it out,' said Dad.

Griff punched me on my leg and then folded his arms and stared out of the window. Just like butter wouldn't melt in his birthday-boy mouth. In my head, I grabbed him by the wrist, twisted his arm behind his back and made him squeak like a guinea pig. But I didn't do it for real. I didn't have the energy. Instead I said, 'Dad, will you please turn the air con up? It's like a sauna in here and it's turning Griff into a total dick.'

7

'Shut up,' said Griff. 'You can't speak to me like that – it's my *birthday*!' Sticking his face through the front headrests, he said, 'Did you hear that?'

'Hear what?' said Dad.

I laughed at having got away with it, and then I put my face right up close to Griff's and started singing, 'Happy Birthday to yah . . . happy birrrrrthday!' And singing that song reminded me of my *own* birthday just a few weeks earlier and how I'd taken Matilda Sommer to a house party and how – at last – I'd got to kiss her. I put my mouth by Griff's ear and whispered, 'Thirteen and I bet you've never had a snog, have you, Dickie-boy?'

Griff shouted, 'Shut up, and I am *not* a dick!'

Mum said, 'Can we *please* stop saying "dick"?'

I could see Dad looking at my brother in the rear-view mirror. 'We should've left you in Barcelona. Why didn't we do that?'

'Ha ha ha,' said Griff. 'If you weren't so mean with the air conditioning, we wouldn't even be having this conversation.'

'Hey,' said Dad. 'How am I mean? I've just taken you on a ten-day road trip of New England. That's all my savings gone in one go. And anyway, it's not about saving *money*, it's about saving the *planet*. I don't see the point of burning more fuel than we need to.'

'That's so stupid,' said Griff.

I lifted up my leg and kicked him. 'It's not stupid, you

idiot.' Then I looked at the back of my dad's head and said, 'So can we open the windows instead?'

'OK, fine,' said Dad. 'Have it your way. But in that case I'm turning the air con right off. There's no point having it on unless the windows are shut.'

Me and Griff both groaned. In spite of a few wobbles, me and my brother have always had a connection as strong as a cosmic force. And now it was back. Us against Dad.

Dad's hand hovered in front of the dashboard. 'On or off?'

'On,' I muttered.

'Leave it on,' said Griff.

Turning away, I rested my forehead against the glass of my closed window. Outside, the highway was getting more and more rammed with cars. It was like a big rude reminder that our holiday was over.

But what a holiday it had been.

We'd hired a racing-green Mini Cooper with white speed stripes that Dad reckoned was the coolest car on the road. We'd been to the Catskill Mountains – Dad's choice – and swum in an actual Swan Lake – Mum's choice – and visited an ice-cream factory in Vermont where we'd tasted honey jalapeño ice cream. And then we'd driven to Massachusetts and kicked a ball about on Boston Common and seen the Red Sox play basketball and eaten doughnuts by the Atlantic Ocean. We'd had the best time ever.

But now we were neither here nor there. Not on holiday and not quite home. And on either side of us was a solid line of slow-moving traffic.

Even my elbows were hot. I opened my mouth to moan but, as usual, Griff got there first. He flopped his head back against his headrest and said, 'I'm actually going to die. Someone give me a cold beer.'

Mum twisted around in her seat. 'Fat chance of that,' she said. 'You're *thirteen*.'

Dad's sunglasses flashed in the mirror. 'You can have one when we get home,' he said. And then he looked at Mum and said, 'Oh, come on, Meg – it's his *birthday*.'

'Boom,' said Griff.

Mum gave my dad a death glare but said nothing. I didn't either. It was too hot and I wasn't fussed on beer anyway. I had some once at a house party. It tasted like bog water.

In the outside lane, a car the size of a tank overtook us. I imagined the people inside sitting in acres of legroom and ice-chilled comfort. I shuffled my feet around in a space the size of a peanut and tried to remember that our car was cool. But it was getting harder. When you're fifteen and your legs are so stiff that they feel like they are going to snap off, the novelty of a hired Mini Cooper starts to wear thin. And if my legs ached, Griff's *definitely* did. Because my so-called little brother was already taller than me. Only slightly, but still.

Griff kicked off his flip-flops, lifted his feet up onto

the seat and sat with his knees up around his ears like a locust. 'I want to get back and see what birthday cards I got,' he said.

'We're almost there,' said Dad. 'This is Queens. Next borough is Brooklyn.'

I grabbed hold of Griff's big toe and squeezed it. 'You know what cards you'll get. Same as you ever get. You'll get one from Matilda –'

'You LOVE her,' said Griff, suddenly. 'You LOVE her – *arrrrghh – get off*!'

I kept on squeezing his toe and continued talking as if I hadn't been interrupted. '. . . and Sven and Silke and one from Emilio in Spain and a card from Granddad and a card from Mum's cousin Dee.'

Griff kicked my hand away and whispered, 'With a book token inside that we can't even spend.'

'I heard that,' said Mum from the front. 'It's good of Dee to even remember you.'

Griff yawned and then he rolled his eyes. 'This highway is *such* a dick.'

'*Motorway*,' I said. 'We're British, remember?' But even so, he had a point. And we were crawling along so slowly that I could've walked quicker. Our Mini was stuck behind a filthy great car-carrier loaded up with brand-new hatchbacks and even the slow lane was moving faster than us. 'Can't see the world for all of the traffic,' I said to myself. To nobody.

11

But my mum heard. She turned her head and then she wriggled around in her seat so she could see me better. And finally, as the car kept taking us closer to home, she said, 'When did you suddenly get so grown-up, Dylan Thomas Taylor?'

'*Someone* has to be grown-up in this family,' I said. And I forgot how sweaty and fed-up I was and smiled back at her. I couldn't help it. She looked so young and so pretty sitting there in the front seat next to my dad. And she was cool too – with her long hair and her limited-edition Welsh accent and that shiny silver stud in her nose. And to be fair, even Dad looked good. With his sideburns and his polo shirt and his cheap expensive sunglasses, he looked like he was in Blur or Oasis.

So OK – they weren't like most mums and dads. And they didn't have a marriage certificate or a car of their own or neighbours they'd known for years or family who came to visit. But so what? They didn't need any of that. They had us. Me and Griff.

Mum reached out and stroked my sweaty hair. 'I named you after a famous poet, Dyl, and I sometimes think you got a lot more than just his name.'

Dad took his eyes off the road and looked at her with fake horror. 'What is this, Meg? A confession?'

Mum laughed. 'Don't be daft, Steve,' she said. 'You only have to look at him to see he's your boy. But he doesn't act like you. He's so deep he could be a poet. And he's

12

even got the same red hair as Dylan Thomas.' She took hold of a strand of my hair and tugged it gently. 'I'd love to know what's going on inside that handsome head of yours.'

Next to me, Griff Rhys Taylor pulled a face and pretended to crack a fart. My brother was *not* named after a poet. He was named after Gruff Rhys – the singer from some band called Super Furry Animals. Or he *almost* was. My parents hadn't bothered to check the spelling.

'Actually,' I said, 'I was thinking that I'd like us to stay in New York forever. I'm fed up of moving.'

Mum looked thoughtful and then she smiled. 'Well, maybe we will then.' She looked at Dad. 'What do you reckon, Steve? Have we seen enough of this big wide world yet? Is it time to settle down?'

Dad shrugged. 'It's your call, Meg. If you want to stay, we'll stay. If you want to move, we'll move. Wherever you are is wherever I am.' And then he took his eyes off the road again and turned to kiss our mum right on the mouth.

Me and Griff both clapped our hands over our eyes and screamed.

'Break it up,' shouted Griff. 'I'm gonna vom.'

'It's OK,' said Dad. 'You can open your eyes – it's over.' And then he said to Mum, 'Let's wait until they're not around?'

Griff and me practically puked.

Mum and Dad burst out laughing. And even though it was hot and boring, we did too. Sometimes it's easier just to join in.

I looked back at the road. The traffic was moving a bit faster. We were still trailing the great big car-carrier, but more of a gap had opened up between us and it. I don't know why but I was glad. Overhead, a sign on a metal railing said 'BROOKLYN' and 'STATEN ISLAND'. I smiled. If the traffic kept flowing we'd be home in half an hour.

Some music started playing, catching me by surprise. Like the air con, the radio had been on so low I'd forgotten it was there. Mum reached out a finger and pressed the volume button. 'I love this one,' she said.

One Direction.

I shook my head. 'That's just wrong.'

'That's just wrong,' said Griff.

Mum lifted her arms above her head and started chair-dancing. Worse, she started singing along.

Griff leaned forward. 'Do you have to?'

Mum tipped back her head, closed her eyes and sang louder.

Griff said, 'Dad, does she have to?'

Dad laughed. 'You think I can stop her? Anyway, it's quite catchy this one. "The story of my wife . . ." And *he* started singing as well.

Griff put his hands over his ears and started yelling out

the words to 'Smells Like Teen Spirit'. My brother is a massive muso. He really likes grunge and garage punk and indie rock. He even likes old stuff like Oasis and Blur and the Beatles and the Beach Boys. We both do. We got it from our dad.

'Make this end,' I muttered. And then, for some reason, I looked around. In the next lane, a big bald guy was sitting in a white van with his elbow sticking out of the window. He was moving even slower than we were and *he* wasn't stuck behind a car-carrier. As we went past him, he turned and looked at us. I think he laughed.

'Will you all cut it out?' I said. 'People are staring.'

My dad stopped being Harry Styles just long enough to laugh and say something – but whatever it was, I missed it. Something in front of us had caught my eye. A flash of something shiny in the sunlight. A bolt or a screw or a rod or a pin. Some tiny fast-moving thing that didn't make sense.

And straight away a very weird thing happened. My head instantly separated into two parts. It's like I had a split screen in there or two brains or something. And one of those brains was thinking, *I don't like the look of that*, while the other was still lagging behind and trying to work it out. And I was about to say something. I really was. I was about to say, Watch it! or Look out! or What the heck was that? But as usual, I didn't get my words out fast enough.

Griff said, 'I WANT *OUT* OF THIS EM-BARRASSING FAMILY.'

And then he screamed.

We all did.

And the world went completely dark as the car-carrier lost its cargo and a brand-new hatchback came crashing down on top of us.

II

And that was that.

Everything freezes like a film on pause and nothing will ever be the same again because of a loose bolt on the back of a car-carrier.

I'm not going into any high-definition detail and I'm not going to overanalyse it. It was just a freak twist of fate and the odds of it happening were stacked a billion to one against. But it happened anyway. Statistically, there'd have been more chance of us being set upon by sharks or flattened by falling coconuts.

Wrong time.

Wrong place.

End of.

Move on.

I know this probably makes me sound cold and weird and I'm sorry. But to be honest, I'm not sure how else I should behave. I either deal with it like this or I sit in a corner and cry forever. And maybe throw things around and smash stuff up. And perhaps get myself stuck in a moment I really don't want to get stuck in. And what would be the point of that? What good would it do? It wouldn't make things better and it wouldn't put things back to how they were.

So let me keep it simple:

Our car was completely trashed with us inside it. It was like watching a sick flick and suddenly realising I had a starring role.

And obviously I didn't want to be there. And obviously I didn't want it to be real. And if I could, I'd have picked up a remote control, pressed POWER and switched the whole horrible thing off. And then I'd have run off to the nearest faraway place and stayed there forever.

But I couldn't do that.

Because there were other people in that film with me. Other people in that car.

And one of them needed me.

2

I rubbed my dry eyes and stared in dazed disbelief around the room. Cream walls. Tiled floor. A window half hidden by a blind. And random bits of medical equipment. It was hard to take it all in. It was hard to believe that this was happening to us. To *me*.

Griff was asleep on a narrow bed, his upper body raised so that he was almost sitting. He had a bandage wrapped around his head and another around his left hand. From that second bandage, a thin bendy tube snaked out until it connected to a clear polythene packet hanging from a metal pole by the side of his bed. In the packet was some sort of fluid.

'That better be cold beer,' I said. To Griff. To nobody. I don't know why I was whispering because there was no one listening. But hospitals are like that. They make you want to whisper even when you don't need to.

I lifted my feet onto the seat of my plastic chair and sat with my knees up around my ears. Like a locust. Like Griff had been sitting at that moment when the world changed. And then – just for the sake of saying something – I added, 'I reckon it *is* beer in that bag, Griff. Birthday beer. I reckon you're going to wake up as drunk as a skunk and sweating your fanny off.'

For a moment, I might even have laughed. But then I looked back at the bag and went cold again. Obviously I knew it *wasn't* beer. Even a close encounter with a car-carrier couldn't make me seriously think that. And anyway, the stuff inside wasn't the right colour. In fact, it wasn't *any* colour. And Griff's face didn't seem to have any colour to it either. Or nowhere near enough. Even with his holiday tan, he was still too pale. And he had a few strange scrapes and scratches on his forehead and cheeks and chin. And there were some sore-looking marks on his arms. But other than that he actually didn't look too terrible.

Considering.

But then again, I'd come from where he'd just been and, somehow, I had barely a scrape or a scratch or a mark on me.

'Jeez,' I said, and my voice sounded weird in the alien room. I hugged my legs and shivered. The hospital was so cool that it was actually bordering on cold. It almost felt like an unfunny joke. Rubbing the goosebumps on my arms, I whispered, 'Come on, Griff. Wake up.'

From the corner of my eye, I was aware of a blue uniform. Someone else had entered the room. Someone wearing the sort of shoes that make no sound. I turned to see who it was and felt myself lift a little when I saw it was Angelo. Angelo was *my* nurse. Or was he my support worker? I couldn't remember exactly what he'd called himself. But he was dressed in hospital uniform just like everyone else – except for some reason his uniform was a bit retro. I suppose he must have been somewhere else on the day they gave out the new ones. Angelo was young and black with a super-skinny moustache, a tramline in one eyebrow and a fuzz of beard hanging off his chin. Even though I wasn't in any kind of mood for making friends, I liked him. There was something about him that made me feel ever so slightly less scared. He'd been there from the beginning and told me his name and told me not to panic, and now he kept popping his head around the door of Griff's room just to check I was OK. I suppose you could say he'd taken me under his wing. I was glad the job had been given to someone nice.

Angelo looked at a little watch face which was pinned upside down onto the blue cotton of his shirt and frowned. Then he looked back at me and his eyes were so intense they seemed to be staring straight into my soul. 'He *will* wake up,' he said. 'You got my word on that. He's just sleeping off the meds he got given by the paramedics.'

A blurry picture of Griff surrounded by rescue workers

came back to me. Griff had been dazed and confused and he hadn't wanted to get in the ambulance. At one point, he'd got so upset I thought he was going to punch someone in the head. When had that been? A couple of hours ago? Three hours ago? Four? Even though I was numb all over, I felt a pain shoot through me. Closing my eyes, I pushed the picture away. Then I hugged my legs tighter and shivered.

Angelo knelt down next to my chair. 'Hey, Dylan, look at me,' he said.

I tore my eyes away from my brother and did as I was told.

Angelo's brown eyes looked straight into mine. 'I'm promising you, kid, your brother . . . he's gonna be OK. He'll probably have concussion for a while, and . . . yeah . . . he's gonna be upset and unhappy and in shock. Like you clearly are now, ain't that so? But other than that, Griff is gonna be just fine. His test results are all good. They did a CAT scan and it's good news all the way. Now, you just need to be patient and give him a little time to sleep.' He looked down at his watch, tapped it with his finger and frowned again.

I turned Angelo's words over in my head but I was finding it hard to get a grip on what he was saying.

Cat scan? Scan for a cat?

Everything felt unreal. Lowering my face into my hands, I squeezed my eyes tight together and shut out the world.

22

'Hey,' said Angelo. 'Hey, Dylan . . . can you listen to me, please? You aren't on your own. Don't forget that. You are *not* on your own. Right now, you got me for starters. And your brother . . . he's gonna wake up any second. They just gave him a little sedative so he could sleep. That's all it is.'

'I know.' My words sounded weird again but this time it was because they were muffled – my head was still buried in my hands. It was a relief to be honest. The lighting in the room was so bright it felt like it was shining right through me. I didn't need that. I was feeling flimsy enough already.

And then Griff groaned.

'Whoa,' said Angelo. 'What was I just saying? Looks like he's waking up right now.'

Angelo might have said something else but I wasn't listening. I was already out of my chair and crouching by the side of Griff's bed. Griff's eyelashes were fluttering about as if they were trying to fly away. 'It's OK,' I said.

Griff groaned again and started muttering stuff. I bent nearer to try to catch what he was saying. And then – as clear as anything – he said, 'Dylan.'

'I'm here.' I almost shouted it. 'It's OK, Griff, I'm right here.' For a second my hand hovered over the bit of his head that wasn't bandaged, but then I pulled it away, crossed my arms and jammed my fingers under my armpits.

'Hi, Griff,' said Angelo cheerily. 'You're in another world, aren't you, buddy?' And then, turning to me, he said, 'It's OK. You can touch him. Go on. It's good. It'll help you make a connection.'

I looked at Angelo and frowned. Then I looked back at my brother. 'It's OK, Griff,' I said quietly. 'I'm not about to go all touchy-feely on you.'

Griff looked back at me blankly. And then he looked past me and took in the room. The cream walls. The tiled floor. The window half hidden by a blind. All those random bits of medical equipment. And suddenly he looked utterly freaked out.

'It's OK, Griff,' I said again. 'I'm not going anywhere.' And then – because I felt so useless – I stamped my foot in total frustration.

Angelo's hand touched my shoulder and gently steered me away from Griff's bed. 'Yes, you are,' he said. 'You're backing off for a bit. You're very upset. Of course you are . . . It's normal. But right *here* isn't the place to go letting all that bad energy out. Right now, you are so uptight, you're gonna spook your brother. Man – you're even making *me* anxious. And anyway, Eva's back. She's gonna sit with him now. Look.'

I let my arm drop and looked up.

My eyes were met by the kind eyes of another nurse. She had the same blue uniform as Angelo – just a newer version. I'd seen her several times already and I knew her name because it was written on a badge pinned to her top. Eva Garcia. She was young and dark and had all her hair piled up on top of her head. Even though she was small, her voice was really loud and her accent was pure New York.

'Yo, yo, yo,' she boomed. 'Don't you fear cos Eva's here and everything is gonna be jusssssst fine and sweet. Eva's got your back, honey.' Breezing past me, she plonked herself down on the chair where I'd been sitting a moment before and took hold of Griff's good hand. I flattened myself against the wall. Eva was so bubbly and so full of beans that she was making my head spin. But in spite of everything, I managed a smile. I knew she'd been popping in and out and fussing over my brother since we'd got here. I almost felt like I knew her. Just like I almost felt like I knew Angelo.

Angelo and Eva.

The first two people on a whole new planet.

'Griff,' barked Eva. 'Griff, open up those eyes, honey-pie. Rise and shine. I know you're awake – I heard you chattering like a chipmunk just now. You're waking up, honey.'

Griff's sleepy eyelids opened up again. I stood very still on the other side of the room and hoped I wouldn't be told to go away. Even from where I was standing, I could see the questions streaming out of my brother's eyes.

25

Who is this woman?
How does she know my name?
Where am I?
What the HECK
is going on?

I didn't need to be a clairvoyant or anything. I could read his thoughts clearer than I could read my own.

Eva clung on to Griff's hand and kept on smiling. 'So, honey, do I call you Griff Rhys Taylor or Griff Rhys or just Griff?'

'Griff.'

Eva smiled reassuringly. 'Everything's gonna be OK, sweetheart. We're all here to look after you.' She paused for a moment. Then she said, 'I'm Eva. I'm the staff nurse looking after you. I'm just gonna clip this little gadget to your finger and check your pulse. I promise it ain't gonna hurt.'

And I suppose it didn't because Griff didn't complain. And he still didn't complain when she slipped a puffy armband-thing onto his arm and pumped it up.

I stood where I was. Rooted to the spot, unable to speak and unable to tear my eyes away. It was like I was watching a film again.

I felt Angelo's hand on my shoulder. 'Dylan, it's time to take a break,' he said. 'You don't need to be here.' And then he smiled awkwardly and added, 'Strictly speaking, you shouldn't *actually* be here at all.'

I was about to say something to that – I really was. But like so often, I missed my moment because Griff got there first. He looked around as if he was lost and whispered, 'What happened?'

It caught us all by surprise. And he said it so quietly, I'm not sure he even meant to say it at all.

Angelo and I looked at each other and then we both looked helplessly at Eva. Eva stared our way in a panic and chewed her lip. For once, she seemed lost for words. But then she pulled herself together, turned back to Griff and said, 'One step at a time, honey-bun. One small step at a time. And right now, the step we're taking involves me doing your obs.'

Griff's head relaxed back onto his pillow. He didn't ask again. I think he was grateful that no one had answered.

For a minute or so the room was silent. I kept still and soaked it up. Since the bang, it felt like there'd been nothing but noise everywhere. The whole world was one big riot of shouts and sirens and voices and ambulance engines and alarms and buzzes and bleeps and elevator bells and footsteps and ringtones and whispers and trolley wheels and gurgling coffee machines. And it was all set to a background beat of seven billion different people breathing.

Too many noises.

And all of them way too loud.

Eva took the clip off my brother's finger and the puffy black armband off his arm. A pen came out of her pocket. A clipboard appeared. She wrote something down and then she broke the precious silence in the room. 'Blood pressure's a little low.'

'Yeah, but that's not unusual,' said Angelo.

'It's to be expected,' said Eva. She smiled at Griff. 'And your pulse is just fine.'

'That's good,' I said.

'That's great,' said Eva.

And suddenly Griff smiled. The impact was immediate. All three of us instantly beamed back at him.

Angelo said, 'That's my man!'

'It's gonna be OK,' I said.

And Eva patted him on the arm and said, 'Believe me, sugar, Lady Luck was looking out for you today.'

But then her face froze with her smile still stuck to it.

And despite the bright lights in the room and the foggy feeling which I couldn't quite shake off, I saw it – I saw her smile crack. It was like looking at someone who'd just dropped their iPhone down a drain. And Griff saw it too. Because he started to cry. It made me want to smash my fist into the wall.

Quick as a flash, Eva said, 'But here's me talking too much and I guess you aren't feeling too hot, huh?'

'No,' whispered Griff.

Angelo lay his hand on my shoulder again. 'Come on,

kid,' he said. 'I know you wanna be with your brother 24/7, but standing here like you're on sentry duty isn't good for him *or* you. You both need a little time to take things in and adjust.'

'I'm not moving,' I said firmly. And I nodded towards Griff. Eva was holding his hand again and stroking his fingers with her thumb. 'Do you know where you are, honey?'

'In hospital.'

We all nodded.

'That's right,' said Eva. 'You came in about three hours ago. You've had a bit of a bang on the head, but we're all here to help you and everything's gonna be OK.'

Griff stared at her blankly.

'I know it doesn't feel like three hours,' I said.

Angelo tapped the watch face on his shirt. 'Time doesn't always tick along like you expect it to.'

Griff lifted his left hand a little and looked at it. 'What's this tube for?'

'Cold beer,' I said.

'It's not cold beer,' said Angelo.

'It's giving you fluid,' said Eva. 'Stops you drying up and feeling bleurrrgh. But once you're properly awake, we won't need that. I don't think you're gonna be in here too long anyway. That bump on your head isn't looking so bad.'

'Good,' I said, and I gave him a thumbs up.

Griff lifted up the thumb of his good hand and croaked, 'Good.'

Eva said, 'You feeling thirsty, sweetheart?'

Griff nodded. Eva stood up. 'I'll pop to the freezer and get you a popsicle. I'll be right back. But I don't want you getting up to any shenanigans while I'm gone.' And then she went – taking all her bubbliness and beans with her.

'Come on,' said Angelo. 'Say bye to him. You're taking a break . . . just for a little bit. No arguments.'

And this time I was ready to do as I was told. I was completely worn out. I stepped forward again, crouched down so that my eyes were level with Griff's and said, 'I'll be back in a bit, bruv. I promise. Don't worry.'

But Griff didn't answer. The meds were still moving through his system and he was already drifting back to sleep.

And suddenly I wanted to touch him. I *needed* to. So I took hold of his hand just like Eva had done and tried again. 'It's all about you now, Griff,' I whispered. 'Only about you. And I promise I'm gonna be strong and I promise I'm gonna get you through this.' And I suppose our cosmic connection must have kicked in because my brother's eyes flickered open again and found mine. He looked sleepy and pale and pleased to see me. 'I know you will,' he said. And then he gave me a dreamy sad smile and went back to sleep.

3

Griff stayed in the hospital for five days and so did I. We probably should've left sooner, but no one was quite sure what to do with us. And then there was The Other Thing. The Difficult Thing I didn't dare think about. None of us knew how to raise The Subject. Not even me. Especially not me. So we all just hung around and waited for Griff to raise The Subject by himself.

And while he was sleeping, I found a way to make things better. Every now and then, I shook myself free from the constant, watchful care of Angelo and snuck off to have a bit of private space. And instead of pointlessly pacing the corridors or staring blankly at the TV in the family room or sitting − with zero appetite − in a quiet corner of the hospital canteen, I escaped it all by losing myself completely in the nearest faraway place.

It was easy.

All I had to do was think of something happy.

And the first thing that came into my head was the hollow tree.

It was in a park in London. I couldn't tell you which park or even which part of London because I was only really tiny at the time. But I know it was just a typical park with flowers and grass and gravel paths and a duck pond. And it also had a hollow tree. Or it did have when I was three.

It's the earliest memory I've got. But it's as clear as crystal. It was a sunny day and I was with my mum. Griff was there too but he was a baby in a buggy. And as Mum pushed him down the path, I was skipping along beside them. And then I saw the tree. It was big and wide and had a crack in its trunk which started way up high above my head and carried on right the way down to the ground. It was probably wide enough for a fully grown person to step into. It was easily wide enough for me. And before I knew it, I'd wandered away from Mum and Griff and walked inside the tree. At once, the rest of the world disappeared. Gone were the green and the flowers and the sunshine, and all that was left was this dark cold nook. It was like I'd somehow stepped into another dimension.

I started to cry.

Straight away my mum's face appeared in the tree's opening. 'Hey, Dyl,' she said. 'I'm just here.'

I cried harder and put my arms out to be rescued.

Mum said, 'What are those tears for?' And then she stepped right inside the tree too and she was holding my baby brother Griff in her arms.

'Wow,' she said. 'It's *amazing* in here, Dyl. We're *actually* in a tree!'

'I don't like it,' I sobbed. 'I want to go back to the park.'

Mum laughed. 'You *are* in the park, you silly billy. You just found a secret space inside it, that's all.' Crouching down, she gave me a kiss. 'And me and Griff are here in this secret space with you. There's nothing to be scared of.'

And then I stopped crying and smiled. Because it didn't feel scary any more. It just felt happy and nice – being squashed up together with my mum and my baby brother inside a tree.

Mum laughed and pushed me towards the light that was streaming through the gap in the trunk. 'Out you go again. Back to the boring world. It's always a lot closer than you think.' And we both stepped out of the tree and stood blinking for a moment in the sunshine. And little Griff might have been blinking too. Or maybe he was just asleep.

4

On the second day, Griff blinked a few times and then opened his eyes wide. I could tell he was feeling better. The groggy look had gone and that terrible beer-drip had gone too. So had the bandage around his hand. The one on his head was still there though.

Even though it was stupid, I said, 'How are you?'

Griff didn't say anything for a moment. And then he whispered, 'I feel shit,' and yawned.

Awkwardly I reached out and tried to take hold of his hand. But now he was properly awake, it was totally different. He screwed his hands up into fists and I took it as a sign I should let the touchy-feely thing drop.

Angelo and Eva came in together. Angelo winked at me and then started fiddling with his dodgy watch. Eva boomed, 'And how are we doing?' She was even louder than usual.

'Pretty shit,' I muttered.

'Pretty sh . . . shocking,' said Griff, and he yawned again.

'Well, just remember . . . you aren't on your own,' said Angelo.

'Hey,' said Eva, 'you're doing real good.' She smiled at Griff and said, 'But if you keep nodding off and yawning, we'll have to file a petition and get your name changed to Rip Van Winkle.'

Griff looked confused. I'm pretty sure I did too.

Angelo and Eva both laughed.

Angelo said, 'I can tell you two are a couple of Britishers!'

I looked at him in surprise. 'Can you?' To be honest, our Britishness wasn't even all that obvious to *me*.

Eva said, 'You sure ain't American, are you? Rip Van Winkle was the guy who went to sleep for forty years. Or was it twenty years? Well, anyway, he went up into the mountains and nodded off for a long time, and when he woke up again, he found that the whole world had changed.'

Her words hung in the air like a smoke signal.

And
when
he
woke
up
again,
he

found
that
the
whole
world
had
changed.

'Oh God,' I said, and because I didn't know what else to do, I cracked my knuckles one by one. *Crack. Crack. Crack. Crack.*

Griff shivered and something in Eva's expression shifted. It wasn't that her face changed as such – that stayed more or less the same. But it was something about her eyes. One second they were full of twinkles and the next they looked like they were filling up with tears. She shook her head impatiently and said, 'It's a stupid story anyway. And you know what? It doesn't matter how long it takes for you to wake up to all of this. There ain't no rush.'

You need to tell him, I thought. Someone had to. And I was pretty sure *I* couldn't do it.

Eva chewed her lip and looked at Griff. Then she said, 'Listen, honey, there's something I have to tell you.'

I wasn't breathing.

Griff's face went even paler. 'What? What is it?'

There was a moment of silence. The pressure in the room was so tense I thought we all might combust. But

36

then Eva sighed and shook her head. 'Oh it ain't nothing much.' She reached into a pocket, pulled out a little plastic bag and said, 'I just want you to know that you can listen to the hospital's entertainment channels if you like. You kids usually like channels two and three. I've got you some earphones.'

The pressure dropped, but my brother was still in the dark. I threw Eva a look of frustration. I couldn't really blame her for bottling it though. She had the hardest job in the world.

Griff was quiet. Even by sick-boy standards. He rubbed the little plastic package between his fingers and said, 'Thanks.' And then he looked over towards me. I shrugged helplessly.

Angelo said, 'Right, Dylan, I'm taking you away. We need to disappear while Eva does her obs on Griff. You can't watch everything.'

'But I want to keep an eye on him.'

Angelo tapped the place where his heart was. 'As long as he's in *here*, you've got it covered, kid.'

'But . . .'

'No arguments,' said Angelo.

I gave in. 'OK, I'll be back in a bit,' I said to Griff. But my brother just sat there in his bed, rubbing the unopened earphones between his fingers and looking worried.

And then I had an idea. Not caring whether it was weird or not, I grabbed one of his hands and squeezed it.

'Listen to channel two,' I said. 'It's got all *our* sort of music.'

Griff frowned. He looked down at the earphones in his hand and then looked up again. 'Thanks,' he muttered.

'No worries,' I said.

'You're welcome,' said Eva. 'Listen to some music and chill for a bit.'

And then I went off with Angelo and together we disappeared down the long hospital corridors. And I don't mind admitting that I was feeling pretty damn lousy. Because I'd told my brother a lie. I'd been checking out all the different transmissions and frequencies floating around the hospital and it wasn't *our* sort of music they played on channel two at all. There was no rock or grunge or garage or indie. Mostly, there was only One Direction.

I didn't do it to be mean.

I did it to jog my brother's memory.

And suddenly I was back somewhere I didn't want to be. And this time, it wasn't the nearest faraway place. I was

back

in

that

car.

And everything was moving weirdly slowly

but also heartbreakingly fast.

And Mum was reaching out

and stroking my sweaty hair

and calling me a poet

and Griff was yawning sleepily with his earphones in
and
Dad was joking around with Mum
and Mum was laughing
and pulling at a piece of my red hair
and
I wanted to say something nice to her –
something that I should have said while I had the
chance –
but
then
a song started playing on the radio.
'The Story of my Wife'. Or life. Or something.
And my brother's eyes flicked open.
And all I could do was close my own eyes and freeze
because I knew *exactly* what was going to happen next.

In a room in a hospital in Queens, my brother sat bolt
upright in his hospital bed. He ripped the earphones from
his ear and shouted, 'NOOOO!'

Later – I don't know when exactly – time doesn't always
tick along like you expect it to – Angelo took me to that
quiet corner of the canteen where we sometimes hung
out. 'We can start taking the next steps now,' he said. 'Eva's
been talking to Griff. He knows.'

And I nodded my head stiffly and said, 'I know.'

5

The person who came to collect us was Ms B. Knowles, the Principal of Endeavour Academy High School. She was our head teacher and she was also the person who gave my parents the last jobs of their lives.

Behind her back, everyone called her Beyoncé. She didn't much look like a Beyoncé though. If you want my opinion, she looked more like an Oprah.

After a tight hug that took Griff and me by surprise, she said, 'No more of this Ms Knowles nonsense. From now on, you call me Blessing.' And straight after that she added, 'You're coming home with me.'

We didn't know her too well. In fact, I'd personally spoken to her precisely twice. The first time was when she'd shaken my hand and welcomed me to the school, and the second was just a few days before the summer break. It was pretty awkward because I'd dropped a Liebig condenser in a Chemistry lesson and it had smashed into a million pieces. If you don't know what a Liebig condenser is, you're lucky. But, anyway, I broke one and my science teacher popped a hernia and packed me off to Beyoncé's office so that she could pop a hernia too. But when I got there and sat down on the naughty seat in front of her desk, Beyoncé just said, 'That thing you broke will cost the school thirty dollars to replace. Let me give you some advice, Dylan. Next time, take more care.'

And I couldn't really take issue with that. So I'd just sighed and stared down at my trainers and, ever so slightly, I'd made the tiniest movement with my head to indicate I understood.

Beyoncé – I mean Ms Knowles – I mean Blessing – sighed too. And when all her sighing was done, she said, 'You don't waste words, do you?'

And that was the sum total of everything we said. As meetings go, it wasn't the greatest, and when I walked out of her office that day, I was mostly hoping to never speak to her again. So when she showed up at the hospital on that fifth morning, it was a shock.

Almost.

I suppose I'd moved somewhere beyond that.

We were hanging out in the patients' day room. The TV was on, but neither Griff nor I was watching it. Griff was slouched in a chair with his eyes shut and I was sitting next to him and silently worrying my head off. I was just

41

about to zone right out and slip off to the nearest faraway place when I heard the unlikely sound of someone singing. It was Eva and she was doing it in a deliberate Beyoncé style.

'Whoa-oh-oh
Oh-oh-oh-oh-oh!'

Griff opened his eyes and the ghost of a smile flickered across his face. I think one even flickered across mine too. It was impossible to ignore Eva. The more quiet and depressed we were, the more chipper and cheerful she became. It was like she was us in reverse. 'Put your head up,' she boomed, 'I got someone special waiting outside who's wanting to come in and see you.'

Griff turned half an inch to see who it was, but I didn't even bother to do that much. Since Griff had got his memory back, there'd been a non-stop flow of people coming and going and I was completely bored by it because I had nothing to say to any of them.

Nothing.

The police came and asked questions I couldn't answer. A trauma counsellor came and only managed to make us feel more traumatised. Two people from the British Consulate turned up and asked for the names of aunts and uncles we didn't have. And there'd even been a visit by a smart lady in a smart suit who said she'd come on behalf of God. And although the bandage was off Griff's

42

head and he was looking healthier, I could tell that these visits made him feel just as lousy as they did me.

Angelo appeared from nowhere and sat down next to me. 'Hey, Dylan,' he said, 'this person is different. This person is really gonna help.'

So I gave in then and looked round. And that was when I saw her. Our head teacher. Her arms were wrapped around my suddenly sobbing little brother and she was holding him in a bear hug.

'Ms Kn-Kn-Knowles,' sobbed Griff.

'No more of this Ms Knowles nonsense,' she said. 'From now on you call me Blessing. You're coming home with me.'

And I don't think I was ever so grateful to anyone in my whole life as I was at that moment. I got up from my seat, looked at Beyoncé – I mean Ms Knowles – I mean Blessing – and whispered, 'Thank you so very, very much.'

It was time for us to go.

PART TWO

–

Brooklyn

6

I need to tell you about New York City.

It's a big place.

But big is just a word. It doesn't actually mean much. Big can be anything if you don't know how big that bigness is.

So let me try and put you in the picture.

Look at the room you're in. And then think about the building that room is in. It might be a house or a bungalow or a flat in a high-rise block or some massive gaff in the country.

Now adjust that mental image so that you're seeing a great big house with four or five storeys and a flight of stone steps leading up to a front door set high above the pavement. And the house with the room and you inside it is not on its own but joined to a whole row of houses and each one is as tall as the next and all of them look pretty much the same. Some are a bit smarter and some are a bit scruffier and every one of them is old. Most have been split into apartments. A lot have grey air-conditioning units fixed to the windows and some of these drip water on the heads of the people who are walking by outside. On the pavements, a long line of dusty-looking trees provides a little shelter from the sun and from those dripping air-con boxes. But the thing that makes this unmistakably New York City is that every single house on the street is brown. And street after street in your neighbourhood is filled with nothing but brown houses and maybe as many as one hundred and fifty thousand people call this neighbourhood their home. And when you take the subway to a different hood or get on the el – that's the elevated train that thunders along a high metal track from Franklin Avenue to Prospect Park – you'll get off at the other end and see a million more shades of brown stone. And you'll hear music pumping out of windows and see people sitting on fold-up chairs outside their front doors, and in Prospect Park people will be having barbecues and blaring out more music from boom boxes and boys will be skateboarding and dogs will be barking and babies will be grabbing hold of their own toes and squealing.

New York City is noisy as well as big.

Away from the park and back on the streets, you can look down the ramrod-straight roads and see skyscrapers in the distance and the pointy white spire of City Hall.

And if you walked there – which you won't ever do because it's either too hot or too cold and, anyway, it's just too far – you'd find that right behind the downtown office blocks and the swanky old government buildings and the central shopping mall with all its bargain sportswear basements, there are a load more streets filled with a load more houses that decorate the view in all the colours of a brown rainbow.

But this is just Brooklyn. The bit of New York City that I know.

That other place – the one that everyone sees in films or flies to for a weekend and takes photos of – is across the bridge in Manhattan. Manhattan is big too, but it's not as big as Brooklyn.

And then there's also Queens – and that's where I left my mum and dad and where I was hanging around in hospital waiting for Griff to get well enough to leave. And besides that, there's Staten Island and the Bronx.

New York is a really big place and it's got over eight and a half million people in it.

And in the middle of them all was my sad and shell-shocked little brother. And right behind him was me. Doing my level best to get him through.

7

Blessing drove us back to her house in a nifty little Porsche Boxter. It was gun-metal grey with alloy wheels, a rear wing spoiler and zero space for me in the back. But I didn't care. I wanted Griff to sit in the front and I wanted him as far away from that hospital as possible. It wasn't because it was a *bad* hospital or anything. I just wanted my brother back in the boring world.

It was a quiet ride. Griff sat as stiff as a crash-test dummy inside his seat belt and I sat and cracked my knuckles in the back. Once or twice, Blessing tried to spark up a conversation but she didn't get a fat lot of chit-chat from us. In the end she gave up and we all just drove along in silence, thinking about who-knows-what.

Me? *I* was thinking about Angelo. It made a change because mostly the inside of my head was looking pretty much like this:

Griff Griff Griff Griff Griff Griff Griff Griff Griff Griff
Griff Griff Griff Griff Griff Griff Griff Griff Griff Griff
Griff Griff Griff Griff Griff Griff Griff Griff Griff Griff
Griff Griff Griff Griff Griff Griff Griff Griff Griff Griff
Griff Griff Griff Griff Griff Griff Griff Griff Griff Griff
Griff Griff Griff Griff Griff Griff Griff Griff Griff Griff
Griff Griff Griff Griff Griff Griff Griff Griff Griff Griff
Griff Griff Griff Griff Griff Griff Griff Griff Griff Griff
Griff Griff Griff Griff Griff Griff Griff Griff Griff Griff
Griff Griff Griff Griff Griff Griff Griff Griff Griff Griff

I suppose it was because I didn't dare think about too much else.

But now we were in a car and I was feeling kind of uptight about that. The fact that it was a fancy little Porsche Boxter didn't make a blind bit of difference – it was *still* a car. And that detail was jangling my nerves.

So I closed my eyes and thought about Angelo, but that didn't relax me much either. Because, in that weird neither-here-nor-there space of the hospital, I'd sort of come to depend on him and the idea of not having him around was freaking me out.

'Try not to be scared,' Angelo had said to me just before we'd said goodbye. 'You're not on your own. There'll be lots of people who will help you. And sometimes there'll be help from places you don't even expect.'

We were sitting in the corridor outside Griff's room

when Angelo said that. Griff was inside with Blessing and Eva and a doctor who was giving him one last look over. As I'd left the room, I'd heard the doctor talking about the dissolvable stitches in my brother's head.

'But I *am* scared,' I said to Angelo, and I wanted to cry. 'I'm scared of going outside – I'm scared of staying in my head teacher's house – I'm scared of *every single second* that Griff stays sad and I'm scared of not having *you* around.' And then I got *really* scared and felt a bit sick and dizzy and felt like punching my fist through a wall.

'Hey,' said Angelo. 'Hey, Dylan, look at me.'

I did as I was told.

Angelo's eyes looked straight into mine. 'I can't come with you. You understand that, right? My place is *here* – in this hospital. There are always gonna be people like you passing through here – people who need me.'

I opened my mouth to protest, but one look from Angelo made me close it again. He was right. How could I *seriously* expect him to follow me about like a childminder? I was just one more confused kid in a non-stop loop of confusion.

Angelo rubbed his fuzzy beard and frowned. He looked fairly confused himself, to be honest. I guess this wasn't easy for him either. For a second he almost seemed to be totally lost. But then he looked back at me, raised one tramlined eyebrow and shrugged.

'I know it's difficult,' he said, 'and I know you're feeling a bit metagrobolised right now but –'

'Wait,' I said. 'Meta-*what*?'

Angelo looked apologetic. 'Sorry, kid,' he said. 'I've been hanging around hospital corridors for way too long. You pick up all sorts of big words. I said metagrobolised, but what I meant to say was *mixed-up* – muddled.'

I nodded.

'*But*,' continued Angelo, 'it'll get better – it ain't gonna stay like this.' He looked down at the broken watch pinned to his uniform top and gave it a tap. Then he lifted his hand up to his ear and said, 'Time passes, my friend. Listen. Time passes.'

I shook my head and sighed. 'No offence, Angelo, but you're a bit weird.'

Angelo laughed. 'None taken. But it's true, what I'm saying. Even when it feels like you're totally stuck in a moment, you're *not*. Things move on. Time passes. Time *always* passes. Listen.' He cupped his hand to his ear again. And then he said, 'And for your information, it was Dylan Thomas who said that. *Your* poet.'

I looked at Angelo in surprise. It's wrong to assume stuff, I know, but I never had him down as a man who knew his poets.

Angelo must have read my mind. He said, 'You'd be surprised at the people I know, Dylan. I hang with all sorts. Dyl Thomas is *properly* wild.'

Just then the door opened and Eva and Blessing and the doctor came through it.

'Griff is doing very well,' said the doctor.

'Good,' I said.

'His eye responses, verbal responses and motor responses are now normal. There's no need for him to stay here. It's much better for him to go into a home environment. Obviously he'll need to take it easy for a bit.'

'I'll look after him,' said Blessing.

'So will I,' I said.

Angelo looked at me with wise eyes. 'Don't forget to look after *yourself*, kiddo.'

'I'm OK,' I said. 'I −'

But whatever I was about to say went clean out of my head. The door opened again and Griff came out into the corridor. He looked different. He was dressed from head to toe in Nike ticks. He even had a Nike snapback on his stitched-up head.

'My sister works in the Nike store,' said Blessing with a shrug and a grin. 'Y'all lucky she don't work in Bargain Busters.'

'He looks like Kanye West,' I said.

'More like Eminem's better-behaved little brother,' said Angelo.

And for the first time in ages, Griff actually grinned. 'I look like Kanye West, don't I?'

'Ha,' I said, and gave Angelo a look of triumph. 'Kanye 2 − Eminem 0.' And there it was again. Griff's and my cosmic connection.

Angelo shrugged.

But Blessing only smiled and said, 'Let's go home.'

A car horn cut through my thoughts. 'Hey,' shouted Blessing through her open window, 'you boys need to *use the sidewalk*.'

In the middle of the street, a couple of kids turned to see who was shouting at them. I recognised them vaguely. One of the boys was bouncing a ball and wearing a baggy blue vest with the number thirteen on the front. He bounced his ball very deliberately in front of the car and then, together with his mate, did a super-slow-motion walk over to the pavement. 'Assholes,' said Blessing under her breath. Then, louder, she said, 'I know these guys. I think they're in your year, Griff.'

Griff said, 'Mm,' and moved his head in a micro-nod.

Blessing slowed to a halt and then reversed into a parking space. 'This is it,' she said, as the car came to a final stop. 'This is the street I live on and that house just *there* –' she nodded with her head – 'is my house.'

Griff and I followed the line of her gaze and looked out of the window. The house was big. It had four storeys, a stone stairway up to the front door and solid walls in Brooklyn brown. In any other circumstances I'd have been impressed.

Griff unclicked his seat belt. 'You live in *all* of it?'

Blessing smiled. 'Maybe some day. But for now I rent

out the first two floors to Freda – she's a sweet old friend of mine. I live upstairs in the rest.'

I didn't say anything. I was feeling sort of . . . well . . . metagrobolised.

'So this is Jefferson Avenue between Bedford and Franklin,' said Blessing. 'Remember that and you won't get lost.'

I half laughed then. 'You reckon? Too late. I'm already *totally* lost.'

This time it was Griff who said nothing.

Blessing scratched her head. Then she nodded at the steps leading up to her front door. 'Go sit on the stoop while I lock up the car.'

We got out and stepped into the full power of the midday sun. After the coolness of the hospital, I almost expected it to burn me to blisters, but I guess my skin was just as numb as the rest of me. I squinted and looked around. There were Brooklyn brownstones as far as I could see and the same old dusty Brooklyn trees and broken Brooklyn pavements and parked cars by every kerb. And in a basketball court on the other side of the road, the boys we'd seen earlier were shooting hoops. Apart from their chat and the sound of the ball bouncing between them, Jefferson Avenue was fairly quiet. I suppose it was more or less like any other Brooklyn side street. But then, a few blocks away, I heard a loud and low rumble and my eyes wanted to swim with tears. It was the unmistakable sound of the el-train thundering along its tracks. 'I know this place,' I said. 'I know where we are.'

Blessing – who was busy booby-trapping her car with steering locks and wheel clamps – looked around. A moment later she joined us on the pavement and said, 'Hey, it's OK.'

But we all knew it wasn't OK, and Griff was full-on crying. He was trying to hide it, but me and Blessing could see it anyway. Griff rubbed his face with the sleeve of his new Nike hoodie and said, 'That was the Franklin Avenue el-train we just heard, wasn't it?'

Blessing nodded.

'It's how we get to school,' he said. 'Me and Dyl and my mum and dad – from where we lived at Park Slope.'

'Stop it, Griff,' I said.

'We all travel in together,' said Griff.

'*Please*,' I said.

'We get the el at Prospect Park and then we get off at Franklin Avenue and then we walk the few blocks from there to school. It doesn't take us long. I mean, it didn't. I mean . . .' Griff's voice trailed away to nothing. I lifted my arms up and folded them on top of my head and stared hopelessly at the ground.

'Come on,' said Blessing. 'Let's get you inside.'

Blessing's house – or the bit of it she lived in – was nothing like any home we've ever had. My mum and dad

57

didn't keep stuff. 'We're rolling stones,' my mum said more than once, 'we gather no moss.' And more than once, Griff and I had stood by and watched as she'd binned all the 'things we didn't need'. And it was only knowing that we'd get new stuff when we got to the next apartment in the next city in the next country that stopped us from being sad. But Blessing's home was full of things. Instead of walls, she had music and books. Rows and rows of old LP records reached from floor to ceiling on two sides of her living room. On a third wall she kept her books. And sharing these bookshelves were arty whatchamacallits and photos of smiling people and pot plants with leaves that trailed down like green ladders to the shelves below. And on the floor there were *more* books stacked up in low piles and rugs woven from bits of rag in lots of crazy colours and upturned wine crates with candles on. And there was an ancient boxy television almost hidden in a corner. And on a bashed-up leather sofa, there were six or seven cushions and a cat. And the cat was huge and black.

'That's Pudders,' said Blessing. 'I should warn you – she's got a serious cattitude.'

I reached out a hand to stroke her, but straight away she lifted her face and hissed at me. Quickly I pulled my hand back.

'Wow,' said Griff. 'You're not joking.'

'C'mon, Pudders,' said Blessing. 'Try to be nice.'

Without taking her eyes off me, Pudders puffed herself up and made a kind of howly-growly sound. And then she turned around three times on the spot and sank back down on the sofa with her back to all of us.

Blessing shrugged. 'Don't take it personally. She's like that with everyone – except Freda downstairs. I found her half starved and living under the stoop. She's friendlier now than she was then, but she ain't ever gonna be crowned Miss Cat-Congeniality. You'll like Marlon better.'

The silence that followed was the sound of Griff and me both wondering who the heck Marlon was.

'You wanna see your room?' said Blessing.

We nodded.

'Come on, I'll show you.'

We followed her up the stairs to the top floor of the house and along the landing to a door at the end. The whole situation was so weird and so totally metagrobolising that I was having trouble taking it all in. I was in my principal's house.

My *head teacher's* house.

But then again, *nothing* was normal any more.

'That's the washroom there,' said Blessing, a step ahead of me and waving at a door, 'and you're in *here*.' She stopped outside another door. 'It's the spare room. But as long as you need it, it's *your* room.'

We stepped in and straight away I could see it was a much bigger room than we were used to. And on the big bed was even more Nike sports gear and it was brand new with Nike tags.

'It's just to see you through,' said Blessing. 'As soon as we can, we'll take a ride over to Park Slope and pick up your things.'

'Thanks,' I said. And then I remembered how almost everything we owned had been shoved in holdalls in the boot of a car that no longer existed. I looked hopelessly at the ground again and saw thick rough carpet that looked like it was hand-woven.

There was an awkward silence. Blessing sighed. 'I know this isn't ideal,' she said. 'Ideal just doesn't figure in any of this. I wish with all my heart that Meg and Steve were here and . . . and . . .' She swallowed hard and hung her head and tailed off.

Suddenly I was very aware that I wasn't breathing. I sneaked a sideways glance at Griff and I was pretty sure that he'd stopped breathing too. He'd gone completely still. And I realised then that it was the first time anyone had called our parents by their actual names. All those people at the hospital had asked tragic questions in tragic voices about our *mom* and dad, but not one of them had spoken about them as *actual* people with actual lives and personalities of their own. It reminded me that Blessing knew our parents in a way we didn't. As teachers. As friends.

She sighed again. 'Anyway, I guess what I'm trying to say is that I know this is the last place in the world you wanna be right now – in your principal's house. But it's just for the short-term. Until we find out what happens next.'

I sneaked another look at Griff. He'd sunk down onto the bed and now *he* was staring at the floor. Without looking up, he said, 'What *does* happen next?'

'Well . . .' said Blessing, 'someone from the State Department is working with someone from the British Consulate to decide on the next step. In the meantime, you stay here with me. And with Pudders and Marlon.'

I wanted to ask her another question. I wanted to ask her a million more questions, but suddenly there was the sound of running footsteps on the stairs.

Blessing smiled. 'Looks like you're about to meet Marlon right now.'

Griff looked up in a panic. So did I. I don't think either of us was in any sort of mood for more introductions. People were coming and going faster than subway trains.

'Hey, Marl, I'm in here,' called Blessing.

A second later, a chocolate-brown Labrador burst into the room and jumped up to lick her on the face. Blessing wrapped her arms around him. 'Hey, baby, have you been sleeping?'

The dog gave a woof in reply.

'Clever boy,' I said.

'So Marlon's a dog,' said Griff.

Blessing grinned. 'Clever boy.'

Marlon turned to look at us. First he looked at me and then he looked at Griff and then he looked back at me. His tongue was hanging out and he actually seemed to be smiling. And even though my brain felt like a block of ice, I smiled back at him. Marlon stood where he was for a second or so more – just wagging his tail – and then he padded over to me and flumped down right on my feet. And all of a sudden, I was happier than you'd ever think possible.

Griff slipped off the bed, squatted down by Marlon's head and stroked him gently.

Blessing said, 'I'm gonna go downstairs and leave you guys alone for a bit. Stay up here as long as you like and come down whenever you want. My house is *your* house.' And with that she shut the door and left us. Marlon, his tail still wagging, lifted his head off my foot and looked right up at me. I swear to God that dog was smiling. Sliding off the bed, I sat down on the floor with him too. He was like a doggy sandwich with two brothers as the bread. 'Hello, Marlon,' I whispered into his ear, 'we're so glad you're here.' And even though I didn't say them out loud, I added four more secret words of my own:

And I am especially.

Then I put my arms around his neck, shut my eyes and buried my face in his soft warm head.

8

Marlon mostly slept on the bed with Griff that night. I knew there was no way I was going to sleep, so I settled myself down in a big comfy armchair and, for ages, I just sat there in the dark and listened to the quiet sound of my brother breathing and the louder sound of Marlon snuffling and shuffling about. Sometimes Marlon sighed and sometimes he squeaked and other times he sat bolt upright with a jerk and had a high-speed scratch before flumping back down with a satisfied sigh. And because I didn't want to disturb his doggy dreams any more than I wanted to disturb Griff's human ones, I kept as still as stone and waited for time to pass. At some point, Marlon started to snore. It didn't bother me. In fact, I found it comforting. At another point, he jumped down from the bed and sat next to me with his nose pushed into my lap. Some people say that dogs don't actually think – they just react. But I reckon that's rot. Marlon could see me sitting in that chair and he thought I needed some company. He thought I needed it every bit as much as Griff. Probably even more. And maybe he was right.

But at some stage Marlon switched his attention back to Griff and I drifted away again. To the nearest faraway place. And in no more time than it takes to wink an eye, my comfy armchair had transformed into a

long

hard

bench

with a safety bar across it. My mum was sitting next to five-year-old me on one side, and on the other was a little German girl no bigger than me. All three of us were riding on the back of a gigantic swan and the German girl was waving down at her mum, who was waving back and taking photos. In front of us was the swan's long neck and smiling face, and he was trundling upwards on a steep railway track. I sat stiffly in my seat. Then – just as our swan was reaching the highest point of the track – I said, 'We won't fall out, will we?'

My mum laughed. 'Of course we won't fall out, you big dafty.'

The little girl laughed too and her laugh was high and tinkly – just like the sound of a triangle from a music trolley. '*Das ist gut*,' she said.

My mum laughed. 'Hold tight. Here we go!'

And all three of us screamed with excitement as the swan plunged downwards. And when we got to the end of the ride, our swan splashed through a big pool of water and sent showers of spray over the watching crowd and over us as well. My clothes were soaked. But I didn't care because I was giggling my head off with my mum and with the girl who laughed like a triangle. When our swan finally stopped, I looked at the girl and said, 'What's your name?'

And the tinkling jingling girl said, '*Ich heiße Matilda.*'

I opened my eyes and sunlight was pouring in through the window and someone was tapping gently on the door.

'Hello! Are you awake? I gotta take Marlon for his morning walk.'

Marlon?

For a moment, Griff and I both sat and blinked in the strong sunlight of the strange room. The light was so bright I could see floating columns of dust spiralling slowly in the air between us. It was almost eerie in a way – but luckily I've never been the sort of person to get the heebie-jeebies over stuff like that. Something stirred on the bed and sprang down to the floor with a thud. I watched blankly as a big brown dog stretched out his front legs, gave an enormous yawn and then rocked his entire body forwards. And then I understood where I was and everything fell back into some sort of weird order.

'Marlon,' I muttered.

And Griff was only a split second behind me. 'Oh yeah, of course – *Marlon*!'

'Hey,' said the voice on the other side of the door. 'D'you mind if I open up just enough to let him out?'

'It's OK,' said Griff. 'We're both awake.'

Marlon woofed, padded over to the closed door and stood staring at it expectantly. The door inched open and Blessing poked her head into the room and squinted. 'You should've closed the blinds,' she said. 'You'll give yourself a bad head waking up in that sunshine. Did you sleep OK?'

Griff half nodded. But I didn't even do that.

Blessing dropped down onto her knees and rubbed Marlon's face-chub between her hands. 'Have you been good?' She looked up again. 'I was gonna walk him round the block and maybe pick up some breakfast along the way. You wanna come with us?'

Another half-nod from Griff. Another no-nod-at-all from me.

Blessing looked uncertain and tickled Marlon behind his ears. Then she said, 'Good – I'm guessing that's a yes. See you downstairs as quick as you can.'

She shut the door again.

Griff sank back down onto the bed. Then, in total slow motion, he dropped his head into his hands and his elbows on his knees and whispered, 'I just want my family back.'

And even though I'm pretty sure it wasn't physically possible, I think I felt my heart break. Quickly – without even thinking about what I was doing – I knelt down on the floor in front of my brother and placed both my hands on top of his. 'Griff, it's gonna be OK,' I said. 'It's not OK now – I know that – but it will get better.' And then – because I was making it all up as I went along – I said something that I remembered from Angelo. 'Time passes. Listen. Time passes.'

Griff sat very still. Just as if he *was* listening for something. I watched him without breathing. Then, to me – to the universe – to no one at all – he said, 'Come on, Griff Rhys. Keep going.'

And hearing him fight on like that suddenly filled me with energy. 'Yes,' I said. 'Boom! Come *on*, Griffster, keep going! You can do this.' And leaping to my feet, I jumped onto the bed and pretty much spun around on the spot like a crazy tornado.

Griff looked my way with a puzzled frown – which was some sort of an improvement on a sad frown anyway. Then he muttered, 'Get a flipping grip.' And after that he reached for a Nike polo shirt, pulled the store tags off it and pulled it over his head. Then he did the same with a pair of shorts and he didn't stop dressing until he was all kitted out like Kanye West.

When we got downstairs, Blessing was sitting in the kitchen and drinking coffee with a seriously non-standard old lady. The old lady's hair was long and gold with streaks of pink in it, and her face — which must once have been as white as mine — was baked by the sun to the colour of a conker. But maybe I should choose my words as carefully as a poet, because conkers are smooth and this lady was not. As nut-based comparisons go, she was less of a conker and much more of a wrinkly walnut. On her lap was that manky old cat called Pudders.

On instinct, I clicked my fingers at the cat and whistled. Straight away, Pudders hissed, sprang off the old lady's lap and streaked, tail down, across the floor.

'Suit yourself,' I said, and tried not to care. 'I was only being nice.'

'Hey, Pudders,' shouted Blessing, 'be nice!' She turned back to us. 'Ignore her. She's a big fat furry sourpuss.' She nodded at the old lady. 'This is Freda. From downstairs.'

Freda nodded and said, 'Me and Pudders get on like cookies and cream.' And then she looked at me and Griff and froze.

Or was it only me she was looking at?

Either way, I was totally metagrobolised.

I shifted my feet uncomfortably and tried to disappear.

But Freda's eyes were pinned right on me. I'm not kidding. I felt like a flashing target.

'Hi,' said Griff awkwardly.

Freda continued to stare at us — at me — over the top of her coffee cup. It was enough to give *anyone* the heebie-jeebies.

Blessing frowned and said, 'Are you OK, Freda?'

Freda gave a weird nod and blew the steam off her coffee.

Lacing my fingers together, I bent them backwards and cracked my knuckles. *Crack. Crack. Crack. Crack.*

Griff shuddered and Freda lifted her cup to her lips and took a noisy sip.

'So,' said Blessing, 'Freda is a Britisher too. How about that! You guys have something in common.'

Griff and I both looked back at Freda, with her wrinkles and her gold and pink hair, and wondered about that.

'I doubt it,' I said. And although that was borderline rude, I thought it would be OK to say it if nobody actually heard.

But Freda looked around sharply. 'You'd be surprised,' she said. 'I may not sound so British any more and perhaps I don't dress like the Queen or Dame Julie Dench, but I'm as English as either of 'em. I came to Brooklyn when I was twenty-two years old and I've been part of the scenery ever since. I wouldn't live anywhere else.'

'Actually, I think it's *Judi* Dench,' said Blessing.

Freda waved her hand impatiently. 'And I tell you now, I wouldn't live in *no* other neighbourhood than Bedford-Stuyvesant. You know what they say about this place? They say *Bed-Stuy, do or die*. Do or *die*! Whatever that means!' She gave a scoffing laugh. 'Because we all gotta die some time, but that don't necessarily mean we have to stop *doing*

69

stuff. No, it don't! Not if you believe in the *immortality of the soul.*'

Me and Griff and Blessing stared at her in shock. The conversation was going in a very **bad** direction.

'WegottatakeMarlonforawalk,' said Blessing much too quickly and much too loudly. Getting up from her stool, she took Marlon's lead from a hook on the wall and slapped her thigh to entice him out of a big doggy basket in the corner of the kitchen.

'I'm outta here anyways,' said Freda. 'I gotta go smoke a cigarette. I'll catch up with y'all later.' She paused and then she gave another weird nod. 'Look forward to it.'

The second she'd gone, Griff said, 'Um . . . is it just me or is she weird?'

I burst out laughing. It was the first small sign I'd seen of Griff getting back on form.

Blessing gave an apologetic smile. 'Yeah, I'm sorry about all that *do or die* stuff. Freda is sweet and kind and totally harmless. But let's just say she's . . . er . . . she's . . . *original.*'

Griff looked doubtful. 'Original?'

'More like majorly weird,' I said.

Blessing shrugged and gave a little grin. 'OK, let's just go with weird. Come on, let's get this dog on the road.'

I'd been worried about going out. I was scared about leaving the house. The fear of it had been building up inside me like a head cold. But, actually, it turned out all right. I kept

70

close to Marlon, and every now and then – when we stopped at a crossing or when he cocked his leg against one of those bright red fire hydrants that stand to attention on the New York City sidewalks – I'd tickle his ear with the tip of my finger and he'd wag his tail to let me know he liked it. They reckon that dogs are a man's best friend and Marlon definitely did a great job of being mine. But friend or not, he looked a proper fright. He was wearing a sunhat and doggy-goggles. Or doggles, to give them their proper name. I'm not even joking. They were in matching yellow and his hat had a hole on either side for his brown ears to poke through. The sight of him all dressed up was almost enough to make me and Griff laugh. And when Pudders came back in the kitchen to see what was going on, I'm pretty sure *she* came close to laughing too.

'This is a new outfit,' Blessing said. 'But I gotta try something because he's old and he doesn't do too good in the sun.'

But he did well enough trotting around the block with me and Blessing and Griff. And he seemed to make an impact on everyone who saw him. First we walked past the basketball court and those two same boys were already there – shooting hoops before 9 a.m. They stopped bouncing their ball so they could look at Marlon and laugh.

Blessing called out, 'Hey, don't laugh at my dog. You wanna give him a complex?'

'Sorry, ma'am,' one of them called out. And then he said, 'Sorry, Mr Dog, sir.' And then they both cracked up laughing again and went back to being wannabe superstars for the New York Knicks.

Next we took a sharp right onto Bedford Street and it was immediately busier and noisier but also the quietest part of our walk, because our school was so close we could have turned our heads to see it if we wanted to. But neither me nor Griff *did* want to see it. It was impossible to think about school without thinking about Mum and Dad, and it was impossible to think about them without feeling unbelievably unbearably cripplingly sad. And it was impossible for me to feel any of that so I just switched off and imagined I was nothing more than floating columns of dust spiralling slowly in the air. And I kept on thinking that until we reached the busy crossing on Fulton Street. But then I had to pull myself back together because someone was shouting. 'Hey, lady! Stop yo' talking and git on wit' yo' job. There's a short-sighted dog waiting to cross this road!'

I zoned back in. On the other side of the street, a crossing-patrol woman was leaning against her lollipop and chatting with another woman who had two little kids with her. We watched as the patrol lady sucked in her cheeks, passed her lollipop to her friend and slowly turned to face the heckler with her arms folded. She said, 'Are you talking to me?'

Blessing said, 'Uh-oh. I think we're about to witness a New York moment.'

The heckler – a guy with a hairbrush wedged firmly into his hair – threw out his arms and gestured impatiently at us on the other side of the street. 'Excuse me? I believe you *is* the crossing patrol, so, *yes,* I *am* talking to you! And I'm telling ya that a half-blind mutt needs your help to cross this street, lady, and he's being waiting there *all day*! So do what you is *paid* to do and help him.'

'Actually, he ain't blind,' shouted Blessing. 'They're just shades. He don't do too good in the sun.'

The crossing-patrol lady and the man with the hairbrush in his head both turned to look at us. The man looked flummoxed for a moment, but then he turned back to the lady and said, 'There's a dog wit' sunstroke wants to cross the street. Yo' gonna help him cross this road safely or what?'

'Ah, shuddup,' said the crossing lady. Then she took her lollipop back off her friend and slowly – very slowly – walked into the street and stopped the traffic so we could pass. The guy shook his head and his hairbrush and marched on down the street muttering to himself and then, moments later, we heard him starting up another argument with someone else.

A little smile flickered across Griff's face. 'It's a bit lively here. Livelier than it was in that hospital.'

'This is Bed-Stuy,' said Blessing. 'We don't do dull.' And then she grinned and said, 'But I guess you'd've spotted that at school.'

We kept on walking, past all the discount shops and the food outlets and the scruffy bars and the prayer halls. Although it was early, there were already plenty of people around. Street traders were setting up stalls on the pavement and others were just selling stuff out of holdalls. One old woman had hand-knitted purses, and as we walked by she started wiggling her hips and singing 'All the Single Ladies' – just like Beyoncé sings it and just like Eva had done on that day we left her. And thinking about Eva made me warm up just a little, because it's impossible to feel completely dead inside if you remember how kind people can sometimes be.

'You wanna buy a movie?' We all paused on the pavement and turned. A guy who was top-to-toe in Adidas was holding out a DVD. Behind him was a whole rack of DVDs. 'Bollywood's best,' he said.

We glanced at the title of the film in his hand. *Hero Hitler in Love*. Blessing waved the man away and said, 'Nah, man. That ain't my thing.'

The man hunched his shoulders up to his ears and started arguing. 'How d'you know? You seen it?'

'I don't need to,' Blessing called over her shoulder. We were already walking on.

'I got others,' he shouted – but we were already

half a block down the street. And we kept on walking until we came to the corner of Franklin Avenue and immediately that made us sad again because we could see the el-train that me and Griff had caught every morning to get to school with our mum and dad. They taught English, by the way. I don't know if I even mentioned that.

We walked a few steps further and then came to a stop outside a cafe called the Magnificent Muffin.

Blessing said, 'So you want a muffin for your breakfast?'

I wasn't hungry so I didn't nod. Neither did Griff. He didn't even do his half-nod. He was just staring up at the steel tracks of the el-train.

Blessing looked uncertain and then stooped to tickle Marlon's head. 'OK,' she said, 'I'm guessing that's a yes. So would you like blueberry or chocolate or cinnamon or raspberry or toffee or . . . ?'

Griff just shrugged, and I didn't do anything but look down at my trainers and sigh.

Blessing scratched her head and said, 'I'm guessing you want me to give you a surprise.' Pushing Marlon's lead into my brother's hand, she said, 'Keep a hold of him. I'll be as quick as I can.' But just as she was about to pull open the door of the cafe, it flung open anyway. A tiny little woman came out. She said, 'If yo' gonna use that toilet in there, yo' better hol' yo' nose cos it stinks like sheeee-it!' She seemed really angry about it.

I looked at my brother. He was trying not to smile but failing.

'Thanks,' said Blessing to the little woman, 'but I was only going in for the muffins.' She waited for the angry woman to pass and went inside to take her place in the queue.

'Stinks like sheeee–it,' shouted the woman again at the closed door. Then she turned and looked at Marlon. 'That is one helluva cute dog,' she said. And after that, she walked off. And as weird as that angry little lady was, even *she* made me feel a bit warmer because there wasn't any real anger in her. She'd just wanted to warn us about the smelly bog and that had made my brother smile.

Griff stroked Marlon's head and said, 'Why is everyone always shouting around here? I'm getting earache.' He traced a finger down Marlon's long ear and said, 'You must be too.'

'Tell me about it,' I said. Because even without their shouting voices, there was nothing but noise everywhere. The whole planet was one great big crazy symphony of a billion different sounds and all of them were far too loud. Pressing my hands against my ears, I hoped that Blessing would hurry up with those muffins so we could get back to her house on Jefferson Avenue and I could hide myself away in some quiet corner.

9

But it turned out that my favourite place in Blessing's house wasn't the quietest corner after all. It was the room with all the music in it. The living room. It was cool and dark and the blinds were always shut to stop the sunlight from pouring in and melting all her old-fashioned LP records.

'Some of these are precious,' she explained. 'I gotta 1961 Aretha Franklin original which is worth anything upwards of a hundred and twenty dollars. *One hundred and twenty bucks just for that one record!* I don't want it warping and sounding like a didgeridoo, do I?'

Me and Griff looked at her confused.

'Hey, you *do* know who Aretha Franklin is, don't you?'

I looked at Griff and frowned. 'I don't think we do,' I said.

Griff frowned too. Then he said, 'No, but I know the

Beatles and the Beach Boys and Oasis and Nirvana and Super Furry Animals. Dad was into all of that.'

Blessing nodded. 'Well, I got the Beatles and the Beach Boys up there on the shelf too. Look under *B* – it's all arranged alphabetical. But I'm telling you, you gotta big gap in your education if you don't know Aretha. She's the Queen of Soul.'

Griff shrugged and ran his finger lightly along the spines of the cardboard record sleeves in a way which suggested he was very slightly interested. But I was massively interested. I stepped closer to the record-playing machine and stared down at it.

'This is a turntable,' said Blessing. 'Feel free to use it whenever you like. But if you do, try and keep a steady hand because the thing on the end of that arm is a needle. And if you're shaking like a dog in a bath when you lower the needle down onto a record, you're gonna scratch it, and it's gonna sound wr-wr-wrong forever and a d-d-day. You get my meaning?'

'Got it,' said Griff.

Blessing looked doubtful. 'Here, let me show you.' She waggled her finger in front of her shelves for a second until she found what she was looking for and pulled it out. It was an Aretha Franklin record. I wondered whether it was the one worth all the wonga. Slipping the record out of its sleeve, Blessing popped it onto the turntable and pressed a button. The record instantly started spinning

78

round and round. Very carefully, she moved the mechanical arm across its surface and lowered the needle. There was a crackle and a splutter from the speakers and then music spilled into the room.

The effect was incredible.

After days and days of deep-freeze, it felt like electricity was suddenly charging through every fibre of my soul.

I stood completely still and listened in breathless wonder as Aretha sang. I'd never heard anyone like her. She had a voice that was strong enough and dramatic enough and warm enough to wake the dead. Admittedly, the sound from the speakers wasn't the same clean perfect sound I was used to hearing from my digital downloads, but I preferred it. It was more human. It was like Aretha was actually in the front room with us.

Blessing grinned. 'Good, huh?'

'It's utterly amazing,' I whispered.

Griff just shrugged.

Blessing shrugged back at him. 'Well, it's different formats for different folks, I guess.' She lifted the needle off the record and pressed the same button she had before. This time it brought the spinning record to a sharp stop. Lifting the record off the turntable, she slipped it back into its cardboard sleeve, which she popped back into its narrow space on the shelf. And then she turned back round and said, 'Hey, I'm gonna make brownies. Any chance of you giving me a hand?'

Griff shrugged again and followed Blessing wordlessly out to the kitchen. But I didn't. I stayed where I was and just stared at the turntable. I wanted it to spin again. I desperately did. Because, in that moment, I'd understood something that I'd somehow always managed to miss. Music isn't *just* music – it's magic as well. It can conjure up emotions that you never knew existed and give the kiss of life to feelings that you thought were entirely dead. And it's like time travel too, I suppose. It can spirit you back to other times and other places and do it in such detail that you can see the stripes on your long-gone trainers and hear long-flown birds squawking in the trees and even smell the vinegar on last summer's chips. And when all those emotions and memories are being generated by an actual *thing* – and not just a nothingy digital download – the magic is *even* stronger. I looked around in amazement at all the visible music in the room and it made me think of my music-loving dad. And I wanted him back.

I crossed over to the wall of records and then – just as Blessing had done – I waggled my finger in front of them and searched. But under S there were no Super Furry Animals records. Blessing clearly wasn't a fan of Welsh experimental psychedelic rock. And there was nothing on her shelves by Oasis either. I shuffled back through the alphabet. No Nirvana. My finger jumped in a big leap to the Bs. The Beatles. Blessing had two greatest hits compilations. But my dad didn't like hits collections. He reckoned they didn't fill you up. He said they were like chocolate chips without the cookie. I looked a little further to the left and, finally, I found something I knew he *would* like. The Beach Boys. Blessing had loads of their stuff. I was just about to pull the whole lot out when I hesitated. And then I sighed and let my hands drop back by my sides. I was too scared to touch them. Since the accident, I hadn't been anything close to my usual self. I felt all sort of insubstantial and nothingy and pretty much like a digital download. There was no way I could be sure that I wouldn't shake like a dog in a bath as soon as I came into contact with any of Blessing's valuable records. And there was no way I could guarantee that I wouldn't scratch them or snap them or drop them on the floor and break them into pieces – just like I'd done with that stupid Liebig condenser. I stood uselessly in front of the records, totally and utterly stuck in the moment.

But time passes. Time always passes.

And I guess I must have wanted to put some music on really badly. Because the next thing I knew, the turntable was spinning again and sounds were pouring softly from the speaker. It was the Beach Boys.

And as plain as anything, my dad was right there

in the room with me. He was wearing his favourite black and yellow polo shirt and cheap expensive sunglasses.

'Hiya, sunshine,' he said. 'I can't stay.'

'Dad,' I whispered. And I sat down on the sofa because I felt too shaken up to stand.

My dad looked at the spinning record and smiled. 'A classy choice. The old tunes are always the best, Dylan. But I'm glad you didn't go with either of those Beatles best-ofs. It'd be like jam without the doughnut.'

'I know,' I said. 'I knew you'd say something like that.'

My dad laughed. Then he clicked his fingers and swayed and sang along to the song that was playing, and I just sat on the sofa and watched him because it was truly a kind of magic and I didn't want to break the spell.

Too soon, my dad stopped singing and swaying, and squatted on his heels in front of me. Then he held my face between his hands and said, 'Are you OK?'

I looked at him and swallowed hard. And very slowly I shook my head and just told him the truth. 'No.'

My dad looked gutted. 'I'm so sorry, son,' he said.

'Not your fault,' I whispered back.

My dad was getting harder to see. 'Listen, Dylan,' I heard him say, 'you're doing a good thing. You're doing a fab job of looking after your brother.' I sat forward on the sofa and peered desperately in front of me. My dad was still there. I could hear him really clearly. But I was losing all sight of him. The magic was fading.

'Please don't go,' I said.

'You know I can't stay,' said my dad from somewhere nearby. From nowhere faraway. I couldn't actually see him at all now.

'I'll see you again,' he said.

I stood up. Tears should have been rolling down my face in torrents but they weren't. 'When though?' I said. '*Where?*'

But he was gone. And the only life left in the room was the music still pouring from the speakers. Lacing my fingers together, I pulled myself together and snapped back my knuckles. *Crack. Crack. Crack. Crack.* And then I put my head on one side and listened. The Beach Boys had stopped singing and were just playing their instruments. It was one of those songs without any words. And it was a strange sort of tune – the type that is somehow sweet and sad and hopeful all at once. I looked down at the record spinning on the turntable. The needle had almost completed its journey and had reached the last track of side one. Picking up the album sleeve, I flipped it over and looked to see what it was called. And then I chucked the sleeve down on the sofa and smiled.

Because it was called 'The Nearest Faraway Place'.

Of course.

'That's *perfect*,' I said. To myself. To nobody. And I sat

back down on the sofa, closed my eyes and just let the music take me away.

And like I knew it would, it took me to the nearest faraway place. Only this time it was

a

sandpit

in

a

playground.

'Hello.'

I looked up. It was that girl again. Matilda. The one with the tinkly-triangle laugh.

'Hello,' I said.

She pointed at the mound of sand by my knees and said, '*Sandburg?*'

I smiled. This was one of the few words of German I knew. I shook my head and said, 'It's not a sandcastle. It's going to be a racetrack.'

Matilda looked confused. I lifted my hands in front of me and held on tight to an invisible steering wheel. Then I made a *brrrmmm brrrmmm* sound with my mouth.

Matilda laughed her special laugh and nodded. Then she dropped down onto her knees and began pushing and patting and sculpting the sand into hills and mountains and winding roads.

I stopped being a car and watched her. Then I dropped

down onto my knees too and helped. When we'd finished, we each picked up a toy car and pushed them carefully around our magnificent track.

As she crossed the finish line, Matilda looked at me with big round blue eyes and said, '*Das ist gut, ja?*'

'Yes,' I said. 'It is good.'

Matilda lifted her car into the air, blew the sand out of its wheels and smiled at me. And I knew – from that second – that I loved her.

The door of the living room inched open and pulled me back to a different dimension. For a moment I thought the door was opening all by itself. I almost got the heebie-jeebies. But then I looked downwards and saw Marlon pushing his way through. I smiled with some sort of relief and Marlon gave me one of his doggy smiles back. Then he padded across the room and flumped down flat in front of the record player.

'I'm listening to the Beach Boys,' I said – just for the sake of saying something. 'This track is my favourite even though it's got no words.'

And I don't know if the needle was jumping backwards or if I'd moved it back myself without even remembering, but we were *still* listening to 'The Nearest Faraway Place'. And that seemed impossible because it was only two minutes and forty seconds long. Mind you, time doesn't always tick along like you expect it to.

'I hope I haven't ruined Blessing's record,' I said.

Marlon grunted and put his head on his paws and we both sat and listened to the never-ending tune together and I came as close to falling asleep as it's possible to get.

Then the door opened again and Griff came in. I stayed very still on the sofa and secretly watched him from behind half-closed eyelids. My brother had a big smear of chocolate all down his left cheek. Suddenly he stopped completely still and stared at the record player. Then he looked at Marlon and said, 'Did you put that on?'

Ha ha, I said. *As if.* But the words were just in my head. I didn't say them out loud. I couldn't be bothered. I was still thinking about my dad and also about Matilda.

Griff rubbed his cheek and frowned. And after that he came and sat down next to me on the sofa.

'Get a flipping grip,' he said.

I opened my eyes properly and *I* frowned too. 'Flipping heck, I'm doing my best,' I said. '*You* get a grip.'

Marlon gave a low woof, sat up and looked from me to Griff to me again. It was like he couldn't decide whose lap he wanted to rest his head in first. But then I guess he spotted the chocolate on Griff's face because he suddenly stood up on his back legs, put his front paws on my brother's shoulders and gave him a big doggy face-wash.

'Urrrghh,' said Griff. But he was smiling. We both were. Marlon looked pretty happy too.

'Thanks, Marlon,' I said, and I rubbed his head. 'I don't

know what we'd do without you. I don't even know why I got so touchy just then. It was totally stupid and pointless.'

'You're the best thing,' whispered Griff. 'Right now, you're the best thing in the whole world.' And *he* rubbed Marlon's head too. Marlon looked like the happiest dog ever.

Griff picked up the empty record sleeve lying on the sofa next to him and looked at it. 'The Beach Boys,' he said. 'I bet Dad's listening.'

I bit my lip but I couldn't stop myself from smiling. Because I knew that Griff was right. But I didn't tell him that I'd seen Dad clicking his fingers and singing along to one of the earlier tracks. How could I? Where do you even begin with something like that?

The door opened a third time and Blessing came in. 'I reckon those brownies are gonna be awesome,' she said. 'This is one of the things I love about the summer vacation. I get to do all the stuff I don't have time for during term – like baking brownies.' She looked at the turntable and said, 'You figured it out then?'

'Just about,' I said.

Griff tickled Marlon's head. 'I think your dog did,' he said.

Marlon looked up and thumped his tail. Then he jumped off the sofa and wandered over to Blessing.

Blessing laughed and scratched his head. 'Well, it wouldn't surprise me. You're highly intelligent, aren't you, Marly? But I wouldn't have thought this was your thing – I always had you down as more of a funky hip-hop dog.' She nodded at the speaker. 'What is this anyway?'

'The Beach Boys,' said me and Griff together.

Blessing looked thoughtful for a second but then she nodded in recognition. 'Uh-huh, I remember it now. It's that instrumental track at the end of the *20/20* album. You like it?'

I nodded and looked at Griff. I thought he was going to shrug or say nothing or do one of his half-nods but he surprised me. 'Yeah,' he said.

Blessing looked at him and I could tell she was pleased. I was pleased too. She looked back at Marlon and scratched his head again. 'Well, you boys made a good choice. And it weren't no obvious one neither. You don't ever hear this played on the radio, and it's tucked away on an album that nobody ever talks about. But I love it. It always makes me think of the exit music that's playing as you leave the cinema after one of those weepie-happy movies. Sweet and sad and hopeful ever after.'

'Wow,' I said, and I gazed at her with a brand-new dose of admiration. 'That's like something Dylan Thomas would say.' Obviously I didn't mean *me* – I meant the poet.

Griff kicked off his new Nike trainers and lifted his feet up onto the sofa so he was sitting like a locust. Then he lowered his cheek down onto his knees and said, 'Cool.' And I'm not sure if he was talking about 'The Nearest Faraway Place' or the music of the Beach Boys in general or the amazing woman formerly known as our school principal.

It could have been any of these or all of them.

But at the end of the day, I don't suppose it actually mattered. I was just glad that Griff was able to recognise the cool in anything at all.

10

I managed to dodge freaky Freda from the flat downstairs for six whole days before she finally cornered me. I knew she would. I'd been expecting it since that first morning when she'd weirded us out in Blessing's kitchen. And she'd weirded *me* out more than anybody. I know it's wrong to make snap judgements based on first impressions, but she'd totally given me the willies and I wasn't exactly in a mad rush to run into her again. So whenever I heard her voice drifting through the walls and ceilings, I avoided her like bad breath. But I knew it was only a matter of time ticking by before she caught up with me. And of all the days to do it, she chose the day I was at my most delicate.

The day of the F-word. You know what I'm saying. Ashes to ashes and dust to dust and all that.

My parents hadn't made any F-arrangements. They

weren't even insured. I don't blame them though – who wants to darken their own day by thinking about doomy stuff like that? So the US government and the British Consulate sorted the whole thing out between them. They told us it would be a quiet send-off. No thrills.

'I'm not going,' Griff had said through gritted teeth. 'No way. I just can't.'

'No – nor me,' I'd whispered. And I'd crossed my arms over the top of my head to stop my brain from spinning off in a tornado of panic. Because even though I was putting on my finest Big Brave Brother act, *I* couldn't face the thought of going either. It was too, *too* weird and way too much.

All three of us were sitting around the kitchen table. Blessing sighed. Then she plonked one elbow in front of her and cupped her chin in her hand.

'Look,' she said, 'I ain't gonna sit here and tell you what you should or shouldn't do. But *I'm* going. And even though it ain't gonna be an easy experience, it would worry me for the rest of my days if I *didn't* go.' She lifted her head and gave a sad shrug. 'So it's entirely up to you, and I'm good with whatever you decide – but I'd really appreciate your company.' Propping her face up on her fist now, she gave another sigh and said, 'And if you really won't come with me – well, I'll just have to get Freda to come and sit with you for a while.'

I looked at her in alarm and then at Griff. He was as

upset as me. 'You don't need to bring a babysitter in,' he spluttered. His face was fire-hydrant red and I could tell he was trying not to cry. I wasn't feeling too fantastic myself.

Blessing bit her lip. She sat up straighter and placed her palms flat on the table. Very gently, she said, 'I know that. But she'd be doing it for *me*, not you. I just cannot bear the idea of you being on your own in my house while I'm . . . well, you know where I'll be.'

Griff slumped forward, folded his arms on the table and buried his head into them. I just sat completely still in my chair and listened to the passing of time. I wanted this moment to move on as quickly as possible. I was scared of getting stuck in it.

Blessing said, 'And anyway, Pudders and Marlon will be pleased to see her.'

Griff still didn't react. Neither did I.

Blessing said, 'We won't be out long. We'll go and we'll come straight back. I promise.'

Even though I couldn't see his face, I could sense that my brother's resolve was weakening. But mine wasn't. If anything, mine was getting stronger. The idea of actually being *there* as an onlooker and watching that sad, quiet send-off was more than I could get my head around. But I couldn't explain this. Not to Blessing and not even to Griff. I couldn't speak and I couldn't cry and I couldn't breathe. I couldn't do anything. After everything I'd been through and everything I was *still* going through, this felt like one step way too far. And I was so upset I was seriously in danger of grabbing the first thing I could get hold of and chucking it across the room. But somehow I kept control and just said, 'I'm telling you – I can't do it.'

From beneath his barrier of arms, Griff said, 'Who else will be there? Will Granddad be there?'

Blessing bit her lip again.

I shook my head crossly. 'No one is coming from the UK, are they?' It wasn't really a question. Not even a rhetorical one.

Blessing said, 'Your granddad has been informed and he sends his love – there's a card coming in the mail – but . . . well . . . y'know . . . he's seventy-six 'n' all, and his health isn't so good. He can't do the journey.'

For a while there was no noise at all other than the ticking of the kitchen clock.

I said again, 'I just can't.' And this time I was seriously starting to panic. Looking at Griff, I said, 'I'm sorry, Griff – I really am. I'll put myself through anything, but not this. If you want to go, you'll have to go without me. I can't watch that – *I can't.*' And then – to stop myself from punching my hand straight through the tabletop – I cracked my knuckles. *Crack. Crack. Crack. Crack.*

Griff shivered and looked up. My bad energy was

blatantly bothering him. To be fair, it was bothering me too. After what felt like five years, he looked back at Blessing and mumbled, 'All right, I'll go. I'll do it for Dylan.' Wiping his nose on the back of his hand, he sniffed and added, 'And for Mum and Dad too of course.'

Blessing nodded slowly and I felt her relief wash over me. Or maybe it was my *own* relief I was feeling. It was pretty cowardly of me, I know – but I was glad Griff was going. As much as I was glad that I *wasn't*. Although I also knew that wherever I hid myself that day, and whatever I did, part of me *would* be there whether I liked it or not. It was unavoidable. You don't dodge something like that.

'Thank you,' I said to Griff. 'I appreciate it. More than you can ever know.'

And Blessing said, 'Thanks, Griff. You're a hero.'

Griff didn't say anything. His face looked like it was made of wax and wouldn't move.

I hesitated and then I put my hand lightly on his arm. 'I'm sorry, Griff,' I said again. 'I know it – I'm a total dick.'

And finally Griff melted. He shrugged and the tiniest of tiny smiles twitched across his lips. 'I know,' he said.

So two days later, Griff got all dressed up in a sharp new suit – another gift from Blessing, but not a Nike tick in sight – and was driven away in the Porsche Boxter. And I stayed behind.

With Freda.

I hadn't actually been expecting her.

I thought the babysitting threat had passed. I thought I'd lie on the couch with the record player on and lose myself in 'The Nearest Faraway Place'. Played on repeat.

But then *she* rocked up. Complete with a big bag of multi-fruit hard gums, an even bigger bag of knitting and a packet of pet treats for both Marlon and Pudders. As soon as she pushed open the door and stuck her head in the hallway, I panicked. And then I dived behind the back of the sofa and hid.

It was childish, I know. And I hadn't even thought it through. The Beach Boys were still playing. Very quietly – but loud enough to tell her I was in. Before I could go back and do anything about it, Marlon came and hid with me. I think he thought it was a game.

In the hallway, Freda called out, 'Hello? Hello?' And then – despite the music – I heard her footsteps clip-clopping across the polished floorboards and the sound of the living-room door opening.

'Cooo-eeeee! Anyone home?'

Marlon thumped his tail. I put my finger on his nose and said, 'Shhh.'

Close by, I heard Pudders do a big catty miaow and then the light thump of her as she landed on the carpet after jumping down from her own secret hiding place among all the books. Freda must have scooped her up, because the miaow turned into purring and Freda started making those mad cat-lady cootchy-coo sounds. Then she said, 'Where's your friend then, eh?'

But Pudders – being a cat – kept shtum.

I sat stiller than stone and waited for time to pass. One minute went. Maybe two. Then there was a rustling noise and I guessed that Freda had opened up the bag of kitty treats and was feeding them to that big fat furry sourpuss. I heard a crunch, followed by a *schlop-schlop-schlopping* sound and then Pudders's purrs got louder than ever. It was too much for Marlon. Without glancing back at me, he sprang to his feet and ran out of our hidey-hole to get *his* treats.

'So there you are,' said Freda. 'What were you doing behind the sofa, you daft dog?'

And all of a sudden, I knew that I was being just as daft as Marlon was. Dafter actually. Because he was just a dog and I was a fifteen-year-old boy. Those were the facts and they were never going to change. I swallowed hard. Then, for comfort and courage, I cracked my knuckles. *Crack. Crack. Crack. Crack.* And after that – feeling like a total top-notch idiot – I stood up.

Pudders spotted me straight away. She arched her back, hissed and legged it into the hallway.

Freda was patting Marlon's head. 'What's up with you?' she shouted after the vanished cat. Then she turned around and saw me.

Her eyebrows shot up so high that they almost took off.

I was pretty shocked too. Freda was wearing lumpy leopard-print leggings and a gold sun-top. She wasn't wearing them all that well either.

For a terrible second we just stood there staring at each other. Freda's hand was hovering in mid-air above Marlon's head. I noticed that she was shaking very slightly and it crossed my mind that it was completely dickish of me to make an old person jump. But then she did her weird freaky nod-thing and spooked me out so much that I forgot about feeling sorry. Her hand slowly landed on Marlon's head and she went back to stroking him. Then, very coolly, she said, 'Oh, it's you. And I suppose it's you who put this music on as well. Either that or the fairies, eh? But, anyway, I was hoping you'd come out from wherever you were hiding and say hello. You're the older brother, ain't ya?'

'Yeah,' I said. 'But . . . um . . . what are you doing here?'

OK, so I was rude as well as childish. In my defence, it was a difficult day. Even in an endless run of difficult days.

Freda kept on stroking Marlon and gave me a tight smile. 'Well, I could ask the same of *you*, Dylan. It *is* Dylan, isn't it? What are *you* doing here? Shouldn't you be somewhere else?'

It was a fair question.

I hung my head and felt ashamed. And then I just felt cross and wished this interfering old woman would go away.

Freda frowned. 'Ooh, I can tell you ain't pleased to see me! But you don't need to be worried by me, my angel,' she said. 'I'm a friend – that's all I am. Someone you can talk to.' She hesitated. Then she said, 'And you obviously *do* want to talk to someone. I mean, it can't be much fun for you, can it? Being left behind. Being on your own.'

'Flipping heck, Freda,' I snapped. 'Cheer me up, why don't you!' The words shot out of my mouth like bullets. But I couldn't help it – she was winding me up.

Freda looked shocked and lifted her hands up in front of her as if she was surrendering. It must have taken a fair bit of arm muscle because she was wearing a lot of very heavy-looking rings. 'I'm sorry, sweetheart,' she said. 'But this is a very difficult situation, isn't it? And I'll be frank with you, honey – I don't know what to say to you. I really don't.'

I didn't know what to say either. For a moment it was like a silent stalemate.

But then she said, 'To be honest, Dylan, I don't usually do the talking in conversations like this. I tend to be the person who listens.' She sniffed, took out a tissue which was tucked into the waistband of her leggings – so that explained *one* of the lumps – and used it to dab at her eyes. 'That's what I am — I'm a *listener*,' she said — as if that made sense, 'and I'm from a long line of listeners. My mom was a listener and her mom before her and I daresay she weren't the first. We go right back. It's a gift.' She smiled proudly and added, 'And I guess I'm the most gifted of the lot of us because I'm a *seer* too.'

I stayed where I was, keeping the sofa between us like a safety barrier. I don't mind admitting that I was seriously scared of this strange old woman with her gold and pink hair. She was quite clearly as mad as a frog in a sock. And, looks-wise, she reminded me of some funny old-fashioned sweets my dad once gave me and Griff during a rare visit to England to see our granddad. They were called Rhubarb 'n' Custards. I hadn't gone a bundle on *them* much either. They were tough and a bit tasteless.

Freda went on, 'So instead of yelling at me, why don't you think of me as your friend? We can have a nice little chat. That can't be bad, can it? Gotta be better than being on your own.'

'I'm not on my own,' I said, more carefully this time. 'I've got Marlon.' There was no point pretending that Pudders was any sort of mate of mine.

Freda looked at Marlon and then looked back at me and smiled. 'Of course. Dogs are wonderful company. I never underestimate a dog, Dylan. They see things and understand things that humans sometimes don't. Cats too.' She looked at the open doorway and smiled again. 'But cats are more wary and more practical. They only wanna be friends with people who feed them.'

I smiled. In spite of the intrusion, I was beginning to warm to her a bit. But still I said, 'I really don't want to talk to anyone. It's not personal, it's just . . . it's just the situation.'

Freda stared straight at me in that way I wasn't used to. Then she rolled her eyes and said, 'Oh, suit yourself, Dylan. I tell you what I'll do. I'll go and have a cup of tea in the kitchen and you can go back to skulking around behind the sofa. But I'm tellin' ya, sweetheart, you're missing a golden opportunity. I might just seem like some batty old broad to you, but it could be a long time before you come across anyone else who can listen like I can.' She tapped her ear with a wrinkly tanned finger. 'I get noises in here. The doctor tells me it's tinnitus. But between you and me, it's just what happens when too many wavelengths and frequencies compete for my attention.' And then she winked and went off to make her cup of tea.

Even though I was less scared than I had been, she was still freaking me out big time. And for a second I wished I'd just gone with Griff and Blessing. But then I remembered what that actually involved. So I just stood where I was and waited for time to pass. And without even realising what I was doing or where I was going, I slipped away to somewhere else. And this time it was

an
airport
check-in
hall

and I was six and Griff was four. I blinked in confusion and looked around. This wasn't anywhere I wanted to be. This was nothing more than a distant bad memory. People were rushing past in every direction with backpacks and briefcases and trolley-bags and holdalls. My mum was rushing too and looking at her watch and my dad was pushing a big metal trolley stacked high with cases containing everything we owned. And on top of all that luggage was us. Me and Griff. We were giggling and had our arms stretched out straight as if we were flying. We were jumbo jets.

From behind our heads, Dad said, 'Will you two pack it in? These cases are stacked up like a game of Jenga. If you keep wriggling around, you're gonna send the whole lot toppling. I haven't got time for that – we've got a plane to catch.'

Me and Griff immediately dropped our arms and looked down at the distance between us and the ground.

Dad stopped pushing the trolley and rolled his eyes. 'Look,' he said, 'we're late. We've got to get to that check-in desk. So get down. You're walking with your mum and I'm not going to hear any whingeing. OK?'

Me and Griff looked at him and didn't answer. Who was this snappy uptight stranger?

'Come on,' he said, and placing his hands under my armpits, he lifted me off the luggage trolley and stood me on the floor. Then he did the same for Griff.

I wanted to say something but didn't. But Griff did. He pointed at Dad and said, 'Why are you so cross?'

'Good question,' said Mum.

Dad scratched his ear. Then he knelt down on the cold tiles of the airport. 'I'm sorry,' he said, and he gave Griff a kiss on the nose. 'I didn't bank on the traffic being so bad and now we're cutting it really fine and it's turned me into a bit of a dick but –'

'Excuse me,' said Mum. 'Can you please not use the word "dick" in front of them?'

'Sorry,' said my dad. Turning back to us, he said, 'I'm stressed and it's turned me into . . . a grump. But we'll still catch our plane if we all walk together as fast as we can.'

Griff said, 'Where are we going again?'

'Shanghai,' said Mum, and she grabbed hold of his hand and my hand too and started walking after Dad, who was rushing off with the trolley. 'Do you remember what we said? We're going to China. And we're going on the plane because it's a very long way from Germany.'

We were still walking at warp speed. I don't know about Griff but I was wishing I was back on the luggage trolley.

Griff said, 'Will Maxim be in China?' Maxim lived in the apartment above us. He was a bit younger than me and a bit older than Griff. We sometimes played with him.

'No,' said Mum.

Griff said, 'Will Matilda be in China?' Griff knew Matilda because her mum – Silke – had become friends with our mum after that day we'd met in the fun park, and sometimes Silke and Matilda used to come round to our apartment.

'No,' said Mum.

I didn't know about Griff, but my legs were just about ready to fall off.

Griff panted and said, 'Will we see them again?'

'I dunno,' said Mum. 'Who knows? Hopefully Silke will stay in touch . . . so yes . . . maybe.'

Griff said, 'Will –'

'Crikey, Griff, you don't half ask a lot of questions,' said Mum. 'Why can't you be a bit more like your brother?' And then she gave my hand a secret squeeze. I looked up at her and smiled and she smiled back at me.

'Here we are,' she said. 'Looks like we made it by the skin of our teeth.'

And even though it was a sad moment because I wasn't all that crazy about leaving Munich and leaving Maxim and leaving Matilda and going to this faraway place called Shanghai, it wasn't the worst memory I could have found myself returning to. Not by a long stroke. Because the thought that – maybe – I'd see Matilda again was my first real taste of that thing called hope.

★ ★ ★

Alone in Blessing's front room, I blinked my eyes and felt more positive. And then I came out from behind the sofa and let myself slowly drift in the direction of the kitchen. It's like Freda was a force field pulling me towards her. And I was OK with that because I wanted to make a new friend.

I mean, why not?

Freda was right. It wasn't much fun being left behind and on my own. We all need someone to talk to sometimes.

And there wasn't exactly anyone else around, was there?

I found her boiling water in a pan in the kitchen. She must have sensed me before she saw me because her shoulders stiffened and she said, 'Are you back? You took your time – I'm on my third cup of tea.' Then she turned around, looked at me and nodded. 'Good boy,' she said. 'I knew you'd come and talk to old Freda when you were ready.'

I didn't know what to say so I just sat down nervously at the table.

Freda switched off the gas burner and poured hot water into her mug. 'Forty-eight years I've lived this side of the pond,' she said, 'and I still can't get used to making a cuppa without a kettle. It ain't natural, is it, angel?'

I quite liked being called angel. It made me of think of Angelo, and even though I didn't like thinking about the hospital, I didn't mind thinking of him. It made me feel calm and safe. But even so, I had no idea what Freda expected me to say. Putting my elbows on the table, I rested my chin in my hands and said nothing.

Freda said, 'I've got a kettle downstairs. A lovely Morphy Richards it is. But Blessing don't bother. A lot of these Americans don't. It's all coffee pots and percolators with them.'

I still didn't know what to say. So I just stayed quiet. There was no point talking just for the sake of it, was there?

Freda said, 'I'm sorry, sweetheart, am I boring you?'

She was nothing if not direct. For a second I stared at her in alarm and didn't know what to do. But then I just decided to tell her the truth. She'd have dug it out of me anyway. 'A bit, yeah,' I said.

Freda looked at me in her weird searching way. Then she laughed. 'Oh, I like you, Dylan,' she said. 'I do love an honest soul. And, believe me, I've listened to some real wrong uns in my time, I can tell you. But you're a good boy, aren't ya? There's something nice about you. Something safe.'

I shifted awkwardly on my stool but I felt a bit better. The words she'd used had made me think of Angelo again.

Freda plonked herself down on the other side of the table. 'So why d'you stay behind, sweetheart?'

I bit my lip and thought about going back to the living room. 'I'd rather not talk about that,' I said stiffly. 'It's personal.'

Freda nodded. 'Fair enough,' she said. She shovelled three teaspoons of sugar into her tea, gave it a ferocious stir and took a noisy slurping sip.

I stared at her enviously and wished I could have a cup of tea too. But she hadn't bothered to offer me one and it didn't actually matter anyway. Because we both knew I wouldn't have drunk it.

Freda stared at me over the top of her cup. 'So how are you?'

I smiled and opted for honesty again. 'That's a stupid question.'

Freda smiled too. 'Fair enough.' She took another slurp of her tea. Then she said, 'Have you tried talking to your brother?'

I shrugged. 'About what?'

Freda rolled her eyes. 'You boys! You don't open up easily, do ya? About *what happened*! About the fact that his big brother is looking after him now. I dunno – about *anything*!'

Even though I was weirdly appreciating the chat, I was feeling more and more uncomfortable with the direction the conversation was taking. I cracked my knuckles awkwardly. *Crack. Crack. Crack. Crack.* And then I said, 'Nah.'

Freda said, 'Would you like *me* to talk to him for you? I'm good at that. I could say something discreet to him. Make him feel better. Let him know you love him.'

I looked at her in alarm. 'No, honestly,' I said, 'please

don't. It'd just freak him out. And, anyway, it's all right. He knows. I'm sure he does.'

Freda looked disappointed. 'Well, if you're sure.'

'I'm sure,' I said. And I was as well. Certain sure.

Outside we heard a car pull up. Then the slam of car doors. I stood up and walked over to the window.

'They're back,' I said.

Freda made a tutting sound and shook her head. 'That really was a quick send-off.'

I shrugged and stared down at the street. Griff and Blessing were standing in full sunlight on the pavement and Blessing was giving my brother a hug that looked even tighter than the one she'd given him that time in the hospital.

'Thank you,' I whispered.

From the table, Freda said, 'You look after him, Dylan. He's gonna need some TLC today.'

I nodded.

'I know,' I said. 'He's gonna need some TLC for a lot of days.'

107

11

Time ticked by in its regular rhythm. Seconds turned into minutes, and minutes turned into hours, and hours turned into days.

And Griff and I got through them.

We took Marlon for his walks around the block and spotted the same faces every time. The people we saw on that very first morning in Bed-Stuy quickly became regular fixtures – the crossing-lady and the crazy man with the hairbrush in his hair and the old lady who sold purses and sang like Beyoncé. And there were other faces we got used to seeing too – like the family on the corner of Jefferson and Bedford who sat on the pavement outside their house at all times of the day, just playing cards and blasting Prince from a giant boom box. And other times, we annoyed Pudders. Or worked our way through Blessing's record collection. We even worked our way through some of her books. Sometimes Griff wandered across the street to shoot hoops with those two boys who ruled the basketball court. He knew them anyway. They were called Kayland and Gregory, and even though they'd never really been his mates before, they were doing a better job of it than any of our own so-called friends. Not one of them had been round to visit. Maybe they didn't want to knock on the door of the high-school principal or maybe they just felt awkward hanging out with someone who'd suddenly been orphaned? Either way, they were assholes. But Kayland and Gregory were totally cool. And they knew what they were doing with a ball. They showed Griff how to do bounce passes and blind passes and pro-hops and pump fakes and finger rolls and dream shakes – and while they did that, I climbed up into the shady branches of a nearby tree and sat there like a spectator high in the stands and just watched. Because basketball was never my thing. So why change the habit of a lifetime?

And other times we did nothing at all. We just zoned out and waited for time to pass.

But, in spite of our shared sadness, Griff and I never really got close to each other. It's like we were disconnected. He was alone in his world and I was alone in mine and I didn't know how to stretch out my hand and properly reach him. He was always right by my side and always a million miles away. I suppose that's what grief is – a feeling of being totally cut off from a person you love. Or from people you love. But how do you talk about something so painfully difficult? How do you possibly put that experience into any words that are worthwhile?

And then I found out that we didn't have to. Dylan Thomas had already done it for us. And I'm talking about the poet again, obviously. No amount of tragedy could ever make me tragic enough to refer to myself in the third person. Dylan Thomas Taylor is not a dick.

We were in the living room. Me, Griff and Marlon. Blessing was over at our apartment in Park Slope picking up a few of our things. This time, Griff's refusal to go along with her was irreversible and I was massively grateful for that. I'd have been there too otherwise – poking through the relics of my own lost life. I'd have had no choice. Ducking out a second time just didn't seem decent or doable.

But Griff was adamant that he wasn't stepping foot in our flat and Blessing didn't try to make him, and that meant there was absolutely no pressure on me to go along either. So while Blessing went out and did the hard stuff for us, we lounged about in the living room and listened to the Beach Boys again. And in the kitchen Freda sat and knitted and crunched her way through a big bag of hard gums and that actually bothered Griff a helluva lot more than it did me. But I suppose I knew Freda better than Griff did. And I knew she was all right as well as weird.

And to be honest, I was probably somewhere else anyway – Munich or Shanghai or some other nearby faraway place. I was everywhere and nowhere. But then I heard my brother's voice and it pulled me back into his orbit and back into that living room.

'I like this,' he said quietly when the needle reached the last track of side one. 'It's like the exit music that's playing at the end of a weepie-happy movie. Sweet and sad and hopeful ever after.'

I was sitting high on the back of the sofa with my feet by Griff's head. I looked down at him and smiled. He was flat out on the cushions and staring straight up at the ceiling. I don't even think he was particularly aware of what he'd just said. But it was nice that he'd remembered Blessing's beautiful words. And it was nice that he liked that tune just as much as I did.

But when the record ended he didn't get up and turn it over. He just stayed where he was on the sofa with his arm thrown across his face. The record kept spinning and spinning with nothing but little crackling noises coming out of the speakers.

I thought about turning it over myself. And then I said, 'Are you going to get that, Griff?'

Griff didn't answer. I never really expected him to. The

record kept spinning soundlessly. And then I noticed a big tear roll out from under Griff's arm and off the side of his face. It splashed onto the leather surface of the sofa and stayed there like a tiny telltale puddle.

'Oh, mate,' I whispered, 'it's OK to cry.' And if I only could have done, I'd have cried enough to fill the Nile.

In a voice that was as quiet as mine, Griff said, 'I wish they were here.'

I chewed my lip. Then I leaned forward and, very slowly, I stretched out a shaky hand and touched the curls on his head. 'I know,' I said. 'But . . . but even if they're not *here* – they're somewhere, Griff. It stands to reason, doesn't it? All that . . . all that . . . *spark* . . . It's got to go somewhere.'

I wasn't really sure what I was on about. It made me wish I'd paid more attention in science or RE or whatever.

Griff sat up suddenly and rubbed his palms furiously into the sockets of his eyes. I quickly shifted back and folded my arms. We weren't really the touchy-feely type and nothing was ever going to make that change. Staring blankly at the bookshelves on the wall, Griff said, 'Look at all those words. Millions of them. And I bet there isn't a single book up there that can come anywhere close to capturing how I feel.'

I scratched my head and stared at the books too. And then – on total intuition and nothing more – I said, 'Actually, I bet there is, Griff. There must be.'

But Griff's attention had already drifted away from the books. He sighed, got up and switched the record player off. And then he took something out of his pocket and stared at it. It was his phone – the bling new one he'd got for his birthday. I hadn't seen it since before the crash and I hadn't even realised he still had it. 'This is all I've got left,' said Griff, and his voice croaked a little. 'This stupid phone is the only thing that wasn't smashed to pieces. How poxy and pointless and random is that?'

I put my thumbnail between my teeth and bit it. As good as it was to hear him finally open up a bit and share a few of his feelings, I wasn't sure I could handle it.

Suddenly – without any warning whatsoever – Griff hurled the phone as hard as he could. It flew through the air straight at me and I had to duck to avoid being hit. The phone whizzed past me, slammed against the window and fell with a clatter to the floor. It was travelling so fast I'm surprised it didn't smash right through the window.

Marlon barked and stood up on the sofa with his paws either side of my body. It's like he was using his body to shield me. I love that dog.

From the bookshelves on the other side of the room there was a yowly howl, a flurry of fur and an avalanche of falling books. Pudders sprang like a poltergeist from her hiding place and scarpered.

'Jeez, Griff,' I said. 'Calm down! You're scaring the crap out of all of us!'

'Oh crap,' said Griff, and he ran over to the window to check the glass was OK.

The door of the living room opened and Freda appeared. She looked around the room anxiously, looked at Griff and then – with a little nod – her eyes rested on me. 'Everything all right?' she said.

I shrugged in a gesture that said, *Who knows?*

Griff went red. He stooped, picked up his phone and held it out so Freda could see it. 'I . . . um . . . I dropped my phone.'

Freda said, 'Did you now?' She didn't look the faintest bit convinced.

'Yeah,' mumbled Griff.

Freda nodded at the bookshelves. 'Drop some books too, did ya?'

'That wasn't me,' said Griff. 'That was Pudders.'

Freda raised her eyebrows and looked back at me. I was still sat on top of the sofa and Marlon was now standing up with his head in my lap. Freda said, 'Was this *your* doing?'

'*No,*' I said, outraged. 'I had nothing to do with it.'

Marlon barked and thumped his tail against my legs.

'Not him,' said Griff. '*Pudders.*'

'Oh, I see,' said Freda. 'We're blaming the cat, are we?'

'Er . . . *yes,*' I said. 'Because she's the one who jumped out of the bookcase and knocked all the books on the floor. Not Griff. And not *me* either, if that's what you're thinking.'

Freda nodded. She looked at Griff. 'But are you sure you're all right, sweetheart? I thought I heard you talking earlier. If you don't mind me saying, you sounded upset.'

Griff went redder than ever. 'That must've been voices on the record player,' he said.

Freda nodded again, very slowly. Then she said, 'If you ever wanna talk, Griff, I'm a great listener. I really am.'

'She really is as well,' I said.

Freda's face lit up and she smiled at me.

Griff said, 'Nah. It's OK. But thanks.'

Freda looked at him and sighed. Then she looked over at me and I just shrugged. It was Griff's choice. I couldn't *make* him talk to her. Finally Freda rolled her eyes. 'You boys! You don't open up easily, do ya?'

'I said, I'm fine,' said Griff coldly.

'Well, good,' said Freda. 'But just remember, there's a cup of tea and a friendly ear waiting for you in the kitchen whenever you want it.' And then she closed the door and went away again.

'Spooky old bag,' said Griff.

'At least you got offered a cup of tea,' I said.

'She can keep her crummy cup of tea,' said Griff.

I grinned. Because sometimes things are funny even when they aren't.

Griff sighed, walked over to the fallen books and sank down on his knees. Then he began stacking them into a pile. Marlon jumped down from the sofa to see what he was doing.

'You're getting in the way, Marly,' said Griff in a very low and grumped-out voice.

Marlon hung his tongue out, sat down and looked a bit sad. I went and joined them and sat down next to Marlon and scratched his head. Marlon started smiling again.

'These books are so boring,' whispered Griff. He picked another one up from the floor and turned it over in his hands. And then he rocked backwards onto his bum and said, 'Dylan!'

I looked around quickly. Griff was still holding the book. I could see that one of the pages had got scrunched up where it had landed face down and open on the floor. I bent my neck so I could see what sort of book it was. It was just a dusty old book of random poems by random poets.

'What's so wow?' I said.

'Oh wow!' said Griff. And there it was. Our cosmic connection. Still in existence but slightly out of sync.

Griff placed the book on his knee and carefully smoothed out the crinkly page. 'This is fate or something,' he said. 'It has to be.'

I put my thumbnail between my teeth and bit it again. Then I cracked my knuckles. Crack. Crack. Crack. Crack.

Griff looked up sharply and shivered.

'Sorry,' I said. 'It's a bad habit.'

But Griff wasn't listening. He wasn't even aware of me. Instead, his nose was stuck in that book and he was reading. And whatever he was reading must have been really interesting because I don't think I ever saw Griff so lost in a book in my whole life.

Marlon whined, rolled over onto his back and stuck his tummy in the air as if he was asking me to tickle him.

'Shhh,' I said to Marlon. 'Not now, buddy.' And then I looked back at Griff and said, 'What are you reading? What does it say?'

Griff said nothing. He just kept on reading.

Time passed.

And then he put the book down on the floor and said again, 'Wow.'

I stared at him. 'Wow?'

'Just wow,' said Griff. And he hugged his knees and whispered, 'Thanks, Dylan.'

I sat there stunned. I didn't know what to say. I didn't know what the heck I'd done.

Griff rubbed his nose, looked over towards me and Marlon and smiled. 'I was wrong about the words,' he said. 'There are some that make sense after all. And he was only fourteen when he wrote them.' Griff clambered to his feet and shook his head in amazement. '*Fourteen!*' Snapping his fingers, he added, 'Anyway, I can't sit here all day, can I? Shall we go and get that cup of tea?'

Marlon thumped his tail, gave a big woof and sprang to his feet.

But I didn't – get to my feet, I mean. Instead I lay down flat on my back, stared emptily in the direction of the heavens and said, 'I'll pass. But you go, Griff. And be nice to Freda, yeah?'

Griff gave a little grin. 'Let's hope Mrs Spook is not too nuts, eh?' And then he stepped right over me as if I wasn't even there and went off to the kitchen with Marlon.

When they'd gone, I sat up again. And on my knees I shuffled over to where the poetry book was still lying open on the floor. Looking down at the open page, I saw a single poem written there. It was called 'Clown in the Moon'. Quickly I read it. The title was a complete curveball because it wasn't about clowns or moons at all. But it *was* about grief. And the poet's tears were leaking out of every line. But what really knocked me sideways was the words written immediately *after* the poem had ended:

Dylan Thomas 1914–1953
(This poem was written when he was
fourteen years old.)

Fourteen?

One year younger than me and one year older than Griff.

'Wow,' I said, and I reached out and lightly touched the page. And I'm pretty sure the words crumbled beneath my fingertips. They were so sad and so beautiful.

12

Time passed by in its usual pattern. Seconds shifted into minutes and minutes morphed into hours and hours drifted into days. And even though I was a long, long way from being warm, Bed-Stuy continued to bake and sizzle under the summer sun. And in spite of everything, I knew it would do. Because Brooklyn in July is always hot.

Then again, I could say the same about Shanghai.

Although that's about as far as that comparison goes.

If anything, Shanghai is much more like Manhattan. Approaching by boat, you could almost think that one was the other. The Shanghai skyscrapers rise like giants out of the land and tower over a huge horseshoe of water – and although those waters aren't called the East River or Lower Bay or Hudson River, they might as well be. And soaring above all this – already so high that it hurts your eyes to look up into the sun and see the top – is the Shanghai Tower. And it's forever coated in scaffolding and steel and massively far off from being finished. Or that's how

it

will

always

be

for

me.

Because that's how it was when I was eight years old. A little bit built and loads more work left to do.

We'd been living in China for just over a year and we were on one of our weekend walks around the city. I was watching an old man play with a wooden puppet. He was making it dance on the pavement in front of him by twisting and tipping a small stick that was connected to the puppet with strings. The way the puppet danced and moved was almost too perfect to be possible and it was sort of mesmerising to watch. A small crowd had gathered.

My dad tapped my leg, turned his head sideways so he could speak to me and said, 'Never mind the silly puppet – what do you think of that, Dyl?' He pointed across the street. 'When it's finished, it's going to be the tallest building in the whole of Shanghai.'

I squinted upwards into the hazy sky and saw only the shadowy outline of a massive construction site. It was pretty much like all the other construction sites around the city, only a billion times bigger.

I shrugged and told the truth. 'It's boring.'

My dad shook his head in amazement. Then he raised up his arms and lifted me off his shoulders and onto solid ground. 'You think everything's boring, that's your trouble,' he said. 'You're turning into a right little pessimist. And I'll tell you another thing, Dylan Thomas Taylor – you're getting far too big to sit on my shoulders. You keep growing the rate you are and it'll be *you* carrying *me* soon.'

My mum was standing next to us and holding Griff's hand. She looked at Dad and said, 'Dyl's getting heavy? You mean y*ou're* getting old and unfit, Steve! Remember when we saw Slipknot at Reading before the kids were born? You had me on your shoulders for the best part of three hours *and* you managed to mosh at the same time. And I weighed a fair whack more than little Dyl does! He's a feather in comparison. You're losing your edge.'

'All right, Meg,' said Dad a bit touchily. 'Kick a man in his egos, why don't you?!'

I pulled my dad's arm. 'What's a pestamist?'

Dad looked confused for a second. And then he laughed and was about to answer. But he wasn't fast enough. If you want to speak in my family, you have to get in real quick.

'You mean a *pess*imist,' said Mum, butting in. 'Although, actually, maybe a *pest*amist is a better word.'

122

'But what does it mean?' I said.

'It's someone who's always moaning and groaning and grumbling and worrying,' said Mum. 'Like your dad.'

'No, I'm *not*,' said Dad. 'And that's not even what it means anyway.'

'Yes, it is,' said Mum.

Dad sighed. Then, putting his arm across my shoulders, he bent down so that we were the same height and pointed at the dirty, dusty construction site with his other hand. 'So it looks pretty boring, right now,' he said, 'but if you look again, you might see that when it's finished, it's going to be a real highlight on the skyline. Do you see that?'

I shrugged and stared at the thing taking shape through the dust. 'I dunno,' I said. 'I s'pose.'

Dad ruffled my hair. 'Of course you do. Because you're an *optimist* like your mum and me. We see the upside of things. And being optimistic is the best way to be.'

'And me,' shouted Griff. 'I'm an octopus too.'
And we all laughed then. Even Griff, who was essentially laughing at himself.

A phone went off in Mum's handbag. Mum said, 'Is that mine?'

'I should think so,' said Dad. 'Unless you've been thieving phones again.'

'Well, I suppose I'd better answer it,' said Mum, and she started rummaging through her bag. 'You never know – it might be someone from back home.'

123

'I doubt it,' said Dad.

And he was right. It wasn't anyone from the UK. Not that we knew many people there. It wasn't Granddad. And it wasn't Uncle Dave, who only ever got in touch when he wanted something, and it wasn't that distant relative called Dee who sent us book tokens we couldn't use.

It was much more exciting than that.

We waited on the pavement in the hazy Shanghai heat with half a zillion people and one dancing puppet and this is what we heard Mum say:

'Hello . . . Silke? Silke! Oh my God! I don't believe it. How are you? [Long pause] No way! What? In Shanghai? [Short pause] Since when? [Another short pause] Really? Oh my God but this is amazing! [Long pause] Yes, yes – definitely! But this is fantastic – I can't wait to see you again and catch up on all your news. [Short pause] OK . . . OK – yes, of course! Speak to you very soon then, bye . . . Bye.'

She put her phone back in her bag and looked at us all in happy shock. 'Guess who that was?'

'Silke,' said Dad. 'One hundred per cent. Final answer.'

'It *is* as well,' said Mum, looking happy and amazed. 'Silke Sommer! From Munich! But guess where she is?'

'Here,' said Dad. 'In Shanghai.'

'I *know*,' said Mum. 'How weird is that?!'

'Very,' said Dad.

'They're all out here for three months,' said Mum. 'Silke

says Sven is doing a bank job.' She suddenly looked confused. 'I don't think she actually means that, do you?'

'Ha,' said Dad. 'If only it were true – Sven the bank robber sounds so much more interesting than Sven the stockbroker!'

'Don't be mean,' said Mum. 'Sven's a nice guy. It's not his fault that he's boring. Anyway, he's working for a bank out here and Silke wants to meet up. I didn't even know she still had my number.'

'Sounds good,' said Dad. Then he looked at Griff and me and said, 'Isn't that always the way? Half-decent news comes along when you're staring at a construction site!' Dad looked back at Mum. 'But please don't ask me to buddy up with Sven. I'm not joking – that guy bores me to tears.'

Mum laughed. 'Misery guts,' she said. Then she looked at Griff and me and said, 'What do you think, boys? Do you fancy meeting up with some old friends from Munich?'

'I WANT A PUPPET,' shouted Griff.

'Well, you're not having one,' said Mum. She looked at me. 'What about you, Dylan? Do you remember Silke and Matilda?'

'Yeah,' I said. And I didn't say anything else. Because there was no point saying stuff just for the sake of it, was there? So I kept my mouth zipped and kept my thoughts to myself. And when my dad took my hand and we all walked on along the pavement, I turned my head and had another last glance at that half-built Shanghai Tower. And this time it looked completely different. This time, I could see that the builders had made an amazing start and I knew that it was only a matter of time before that tower stood up tall and proud and beautiful on the skyline.

Time passed by in the same meaningless way. Seconds shifted into minutes and minutes morphed into hours and hours drifted into days. And one afternoon Griff and me were sitting in the cool of the living room and watching a boring documentary on TV about the construction of Manhattan's One World Trade Center. Because there was nothing else much to do.

Then the phone rang. And I don't know why, but something about the way it rang hinted at half-decent news.

Griff muted the telly and we both sat very still on the sofa and earwigged on Blessing as she talked in the hallway on the other side of the open door. This is what we heard her say:

'Hello . . . [Short pause] Yes, this is Blessing Knowles speaking. [Short pause] Yes. [Another short pause] Yes. [And another] Well . . . OK, I guess – holding up as well as can be expected. [And yet another] Yes. [Long pause] Oh really? [Another long pause] Oh yes . . . yes, that is good news. [And a really long pause] And this is definite? [A massively long pause] So soon? [Short pause] Yes, of course.

126

Absolutely. [Medium pause] OK, we'll expect you tomorrow then. [Short pause] Bye . . . bye.'

We heard the click of the phone as Blessing replaced it on its hook on the wall. There was a minute or so of silence. It made me nervous and, even though I was still fairly hopeful that we were about to hear something good, I cracked my knuckles nervously. I couldn't help it. I guess old habits die really hard. Next to me, Griff gave a little shiver.

Blessing poked her head through the open doorway.

'I've just been on the phone,' she said.

'*Never,*' I said.

'*No way,*' said Griff.

Blessing sighed. 'Hey, cut the wisecracks. Sarcasm is the lowest form of wit. You know which writer said that?'

'Dylan Thomas,' said Griff instantly. 'One hundred per cent – final answer.' He sounded so sure he was right I half expected Blessing to look amazed and say, *It is as well!* But she didn't. Instead, she said, 'No. It was another Britisher – Oscar Wilde. Or was he Irish? Anyway, I'm going totally off-topic here. That was Alison from the British Consulate on the phone.'

Griff and me both sat up straighter and stared at her.

Blessing said, 'Alison – you remember her? She came to see you a few times when you were in the hospital. She was with a guy called Dominic?'

Neither Griff nor me moved a muscle.

Blessing sighed. 'You don't remember them, do you? I hoped you would.'

Griff looked at the floor. 'Oh yeah,' he said, quietly. 'I think I do now.'

Blessing nodded. 'Well, Alison has some news. And it's good news. She's coming round here tomorrow to talk you through it properly.' Blessing paused and I watched as her face settled into a smile which was too perfect. Taking a big breath, she said brightly, 'But the bottom line is that it looks as if you'll be going home real soon.'

Griff and I looked at her in stunned silence. In some other orbit I could see that the TV was still flickering with those silent images of the unfinished One World Trade Center. I shifted my gaze and stared back at the screen. The building was half up. But however optimistic you were, there was still a heckuva long way to go.

Be positive, I said. I didn't say it for real – I just said it to myself. And then I sat on my hands to stop myself from having another pop at my knuckles.

Next to me, Griff said, 'Home?'

One single word.

One massive question.

Blessing's face flinched apologetically. 'I mean . . . home to Wales,' she said. 'Where your mom's from. She has a cousin called Dee Ellis? Dee wants you to go live with her.'

Time stopped passing.

But it never stands still for long. If you listen very hard, you can even hear it as it goes by.

Blessing said, 'Dee? You do know her, don't you?'

'She buys us birthday cards,' I whispered.

'She buys us Christmas cards,' said Griff. 'And every year she sends us book tokens – but we can't use them – I mean, we *couldn't* use them – because they had to be spent in British bookstores. We've never met her though. She's just some relation of Mum's.'

For a moment all three of us were completely lost for words. It's no wonder really. After all, there's no point saying stuff just for the sake of it, is there?

Then Griff angrily thumped the seat of the sofa and said, 'I don't want to go and live with Dee. How exactly does living with this *Dee* mean going home?'

For one awful second, Blessing looked like she was going to be sick. Or cry. Or maybe both. It made me feel bad because she hadn't ever done anything except be massively kind.

'Leave it, Griff,' I said. 'We both know we can't stick around here forever.'

Blessing scratched her head. 'I don't mind having you here. It's not that at all. I *like* having you here – and you're no trouble. But the thing is . . . you're British. And as far as the State Department is concerned, that complicates things. And, anyway, your mom's cousin Dee wants you to be with *her*. And she's your family. And family is a real nice thing.'

All this talk of moving again – and to somewhere totally new – was making me faint and dizzy. I wasn't even sure

I could do it. I'd spent my whole life moving from city to city and now it seemed I didn't belong anywhere. Now it seemed that I was nothing but dust drifting on the air.

I started to panic.

The room began to spin around me. I was losing grip.

Then – with no warning at all – the sound on the telly boomed back at an ear-splitting volume. Pudders leaped from the bookshelf with a screech and Griff jumped and Blessing frowned.

'Clear off, kitty,' she said. 'You're freaking us out in here.'

Tail down, Pudders hesitated in the middle of the room and stared at me and Griff.

Stared at me.

And it was like she was staring right into my soul.

'Flipping heck, Pudders,' I said, 'there's nothing to be scared of.'

To my surprise, Pudders put her head on one side and looked at me like she was actually listening.

'That cat freaks me right out,' said Griff.

'I can only apologise,' said Blessing.

And I said again, 'There's nothing to be scared of.' And although Pudders was still staring me straight in the face, I'm pretty sure I was saying it to myself.

Some kind of calm came back. The room stopped spinning. Pudders quit staring. And, as inexplicably as it had exploded into sound, the TV went back to mute. Pudders licked her paw lazily and then strutted slowly to the door.

We all watched her go, and when her tail had disappeared around the corner, I looked at Blessing and nodded. 'You're right,' I said. 'Going to Wales will be a good thing.'

But Griff just sat where he was – as still as a statue.

Blessing shook her head and sighed. 'Hey, look, Griff,' she said. 'You don't *really* wanna be stuck here with me forever. I'm a forty-nine-year-old woman who rattles around this house on her own. I've got no man or kids you can talk to, my friend Freda weirds you out and my cat has the personality of Godzilla. Then there's school. When the autumn semester starts, I'll be working *every* second of *every* day. You'd be living with your headteacher and I'll be no fun at all. I'd be *awful* company.'

'No, you wouldn't,' said Griff.

Blessing looked sad. She walked over to where we were and sat down on the sofa so she was the other side of Griff. Then she closed her hands around one of his – still clenched and angry – and said, 'Try to be positive about this, Griff, and try to be patient too. You know what they say – home wasn't built in a day.'

Griff hunched his shoulders, sat forward and stared furiously at the floor. But he let her keep holding on to his hand. After a second or two he sniffed and said, 'Is that another thing that Oscar Wilde said?'

An apologetic smile flitted across Blessing's face. 'No,' she said. 'I don't know where I got that one from. Maybe I made it up.'

'Genius,' muttered Griff, and he sounded about as sad and sarcastic and cheesed-off as a person could be.

And suddenly – finally – I *had* to say something. Because it's OK to keep your mouth zipped for a while but you can't stay shut up and silent forever. There comes a time when you have to make your voice heard. It's like an uncontrollable urge – and sometimes it's *more* than that. It's a cosmic duty. Reaching out, I took Griff's free hand in mine. 'Blessing's right,' I said. 'You've *got* to give Dee a chance. And you've *got* to stay optimistic. It's what Mum and Dad would want and it's what I want too. And Wales might seem like a faraway random place right now, but time passes pretty quickly, Griff. And perhaps it'll feel like home faster than you even know it.'

Griff closed his eyes. For a moment he sat very still and very stiffly between Blessing and me, but then his shoulders relaxed a little and he sat back more naturally. His eyes were still shut though and Blessing and I were still holding his hands. In all honesty, it was a pretty weird scenario. We were like a chain of paper people except that we weren't made out of paper. If freaky Freda had seen us, she'd probably have lit candles around us and drawn a Ouija board on the floor. But my brother didn't care. He seemed so distant and so totally lost in his own thoughts that I don't think he was even aware of us. Not of Blessing and not of me either. Definitely not of me.

Or maybe I'm wrong about that.

133

Because out of the blue, he smiled.

I looked past Griff at Blessing. She seemed as surprised by that smile as I was. She said, 'What are you thinking, Griff?'

Griff opened his eyes and immediately pulled his hands free from both of us. Then he wrapped his arms around himself in a tight hug. 'I'm thinking,' he said, 'that Dylan Thomas talks a lot more sense than Oscar Wilde.'

And immediately a huge feeling of relief and happiness flashed through my nothingness. Because I knew *exactly* what he meant. 'And he was from Wales,' I said.

'And he was from Wales,' whispered Griff.

Cosmic connection.

Boom.

Blessing looked more confused than ever. But a smile had spread over her face and I could see she was relieved too – probably just as much as I was. 'You're gonna be fine,' she said. 'I know it. *Anyone* who cares about the words of poets has always got a head start. Trust me.'

And from the look of gratitude on Griff's face, I'm certain that both of us *did* trust her. Absolutely and without question. One hundred per cent. Final answer.

Marlon wandered in and gave us a friendly woof. Then he sank down by our feet, put his nose on his paws and closed his eyes.

Griff said, 'Do you need this dog? Can I take him to Wales?'

'Griff, that's not fair,' I said in the startled second before Blessing spoke. 'You can't *seriously* expect Blessing to give up her dog.' But I knew what Griff meant. I'd have taken Marlon to the moon and back if I could. But I couldn't because it wouldn't be right.

Blessing said, 'I'm sorry, Griff, you can't take my dog, but help yourself to my cat.'

I snorted out a laugh.

Griff smiled too and said, 'Nah, you're all right.'

Blessing laughed. 'I don't think Pudders would get past your border controls anyway. They'd take one look at her and see a security threat.' She nudged Marlon with her foot. 'But Marlon and me are going to miss you. We're *both* going to miss you an awful lot.'

'I'll miss you too,' mumbled Griff.

And *I* wanted to join in. I wanted to say that *I'd* miss Blessing and Marlon too. I wanted to say it and, what's more, I wanted to *mean* it. But I couldn't. I just couldn't. Too much had changed.

I had changed.

And the people I was meeting now were just shadowy ships passing in the mist.

So instead I said something *else* that was nice. Something I'd *already* said but which needed saying again. 'Thank you,' I said. 'Thank you, Blessing – so very, *very* much.'

And then I smiled. Because surely there was never a person on this planet more perfectly named than she was.

135

And that brings us to . . .

13

Thirteen.

What does it mean?

It's the number of days we spent with Blessing in Bed–Stuy.

It's the number in the name of a film we saw being sold on the sidewalk on Fulton Street. *Shanghai 13*. Martial arts. Not our thing.

It's the number on the menu that Griff always asked for whenever Blessing popped out to get breakfast from the Magnificent Muffin. Fudge Nut Delight. He didn't say so but it was blatantly his favourite.

It's the number on the menu that *I* always asked for whenever our mum and dad phoned for a Chinese from the Lucky Panda takeaway in Park Slope. Curried samosas. Well nice.

It's the number on the front of the vest that Kayland

wore whenever he was hanging out with Gregory at the basketball court and shooting hoops.

It's the number on the back of the shirt that the German soccer superstar Michael Ballack wore whenever he played for Bayern Munich. It's pretty much the number he wore when he played anywhere else too. I guess it was a number he liked.

It's the number of sides a tridecagon has. I don't even know why I know this.

It's the name of a Blur album that my dad loved.

It's pretty much the amount of euros we could have had every birthday instead of a ten-pound book token. And it's more or less the number of hard cash dollars we could have had instead of eight pounds fifty.

It was the first of three birthdays I had in New York and it was Griff's worst ever birthday, when the whole world tipped up and turned over.

But even then, I'd never say that thirteen is an unlucky number.

How can it be?

It's just one little digit on a never-ending list. It's no more capable of causing bad luck than it is of doing a blind pass or a pro-hop or a pump fake or a finger roll or a dream shake.

Thirteen is just what fills the gap between twelve and fourteen.

Nothing less. Nothing more.

PART THREE

–

Aberystwyth

14

But now it's time to tell you about Aberystwyth.

And it's a very different place to New York.

Although different is just a word. It doesn't actually mean much. Different can be anything if you don't know how different that difference is.

So let me try and put it into perspective.

Think about New York City – with its skyscrapers and brownstones and yellow taxicabs and packed subway trains and elevated railroads and bargain sportswear basements and blaring boom boxes and flat streets and ramrod straight roads and wheeler-dealers on the sidewalks and five enormous boroughs and eight and a half million people including two kids who desperately want to play for the New York Knicks, an old lady who says she has a special gift and one very cool woman called Blessing who really *is* a blessing and who has an equally cool dog called Marlon.

Got that?

Good.

Now delete the lot and start again. Time passes and Kayland and Gregory and Freda must go in one direction and Griff and I must go in another. And as hard as it is, Blessing and Marlon must leave us too. They will become a memory. A voice and a woof on the phone. A cheery email every now and then.

So what next?

Close your eyes and imagine a place 3,279 miles away from Brooklyn. Imagine a little town on the other side of the Atlantic Ocean on the very western edge of the United Kingdom. It's a town which appears like a higgledy-piggledy spattering of lights when you first catch sight of it from the late train that pulls into the single platform of the single station. And when daylight dawns, you see that all the houses in the town are clinging to the sides of steep hills and not a single road is entirely flat or ramrod straight. And there are no skyscrapers or subways or el-trains and you'd be hard-pushed to even spot a double-decker bus but there *is* a huge library and a university and a beach and a busy little crooked high street. And slightly out of town, in a shop on a retail park, there's even an escalator that takes people up from the women's clothing department on the ground floor to menswear on the first – but if the shop's customers want to go back down again, they have to use their legs and walk. And

144

that up-only escalator is the only escalator within seventy-five miles.

This is **not** New York. And it isn't Barcelona or Shanghai or Munich or London either. This is not like any place that Griff or I grew up in. This is Aberystwyth, with less than fourteen thousand people in it. And quite a lot of those people are chatting away and passing the time of day in Welsh – or *Cymraeg*. And it's a language as different to English as popcorn is to peas and one that Griff and I had only ever heard our mum speak a few random words of whenever she was feeling very emotional or she'd had a bit too much to drink.

This was where we went next. And at first it felt about as far away from everywhere as any place could possibly be.

15

Three days after that phone call to Blessing, Griff and I
were standing in drizzling rain by the door of a house in
a little cul-de-sac on the side of a steep hill. The number
of the house was painted in white on a piece of black
slate next to the door. Thirteen.

I clocked it straight away and so did Griff. Putting my
hand on his arm, I said, 'It's just a number, little brother.
Don't let it give you the heebie-jeebies.'

Griff sort of nodded – like I was just a voice in his
head – and then he took a big brave breath and said, 'So
this is it then. Dee's house.'

'This is it,' said Alison brightly – the same Alison who'd
visited us in hospital and visited us in Bed-Stuy. The same
Alison who worked for the British Consulate in New
York. And in spite of her grown-up skirt and grown-up
jacket, she was looking just as washed out and worse for

wear as we were. There was a small splodge on her top where she'd spilt her coffee during some turbulence on the plane, and spots of orange where Griff had speared his drink carton with his straw and accidently sprayed her with blobs of juice. She'd been with us the whole way from Bed-Stuy to Aberystwyth. I hope she was getting paid overtime.

Alison glanced once more at the address typed into her phone and said, 'Thirteen *Pant – yer – Coad*. Wow. It's like a foreign language, isn't it?' Then she pushed the buzzer.

And on some weird instinct, I turned my head and looked away into the darkness and saw my mum.

Seriously.

Just like I saw Dad that time the Beach Boys were playing on Blessing's turntable. She was right there with us. Just for a moment.

And she was standing in the dark and shaking her head. Then, with an annoyed roll of the eyes, she said, 'It *is* a foreign language, you dappy tart. It means the hollow in the woods. And you don't say it like that anyway. *Pant – yer – coad* – that doesn't mean anything! You say it like this: *Pant – er – coyd*.'

I spluttered out a startled laugh and said, 'Mum?'

Griff looked round sharply. A bird or a bat or something flew out from a hedge.

'It's OK,' said Alison. 'Someone's coming.'

A light switched on in the hall.

Mum vanished.

The door opened and a woman with short dark hair smiled nervously back at us. Although she was a bit fatter and a bit older than her profile picture, I recognised her straight away as a Facebook friend of our mum's.

Dee Ellis.
Works at **Cheapie Charlie's**
Studied at **LOL (i didn't go)**
Lives in **Aberystwyth, Wales**

'Oh, thank goodness – here you are at last!' She opened the door wider. 'Come in, come in, the pair of you. You must be exhausted – you've been travelling all day, haven't you?'

'All night and all day,' said Griff.

Dee said, 'Oh, you poor things – you must be dead on your feet.' And then she bit her lip and stared at us like she'd seen a ghost.

I shrugged. You can't expect a worldwide ban on the word *dead*, can you? And anyway, she was right.

Alison stepped forward and shook Dee's hand. 'We're very pleased to meet you and awfully relieved to be here. It's quite a trek from New York.'

'Come in,' said Dee again. 'My husband Owen has already stuck the kettle on.'

* * *

148

Strictly speaking, it was only Griff who travelled all that way across the Atlantic with Alison.

I can't pretend I did.

Because I wasn't one hundred per cent there.

If you must know, the plane had freaked me out. There were too many bright lights and too many people and too much noise. Way too much noise. In fact, it was enough to make me want to close my eyes and spin off into a different dimension. So just as soon as we were up in the air and the seat-belt light had gone off and everyone was milling about and fiddling with their entertainment stations and reclining their seats and squashing each other's knees, I closed my eyes and escaped to the nearest faraway place. And I found myself

drifting

back

to

Shanghai.

And then I was standing on a floating wooden walkway next to a clear rock pool – and I was with Matilda. Inside the rock pool were hundreds of giant carp. They were like the goldfish you sometimes see in tanks, except that these fish were much bigger and not all of them were gold either. Some were bright orange and some were white and some were speckled and blotchy like birds' eggs. We were in a beautiful garden in the Forbidden City of old Shanghai, and it was a place where – once – only emperors walked. But now here *I* was with my favourite girl in the whole world and a fistful of fish food.

'It's good here,' said Matilda with her pretty German accent. 'I like it very much.'

I went red. I always went red when Matilda spoke.

Matilda threw a few flakes of fish food at the carp and the surface of the water suddenly bubbled with big greedy fish gobs. They weren't the only mouths that wanted feeding. A bird – bright green with a punky yellow crest – swooped low, took one look at the menu and flew off, unimpressed.

Matilda laughed – that tinkly-triangle laugh. Suddenly, she looked around with a cheeky twinkle in her eye and I realised she was checking to see that we were alone. My belly fluttered under my T-shirt. Mum and Griff and Silke were just a little further along the jetty and were feeding the fish too. *Stay there*, I said. *Stay there.* But I didn't say it out loud. I just said in my head.

Matilda said, 'Dylan, can I tell you a secret?'

I went red again. Then I nodded really fast.

Matilda's eyes darted over to where Mum and Griff and Silke were and then back to me. I thought my heart was going to pop. I wanted to hear this secret so badly. But instead of telling me, Matilda bit her lip and giggled and then she shook her head.

'What is it?' I said.

Pushing a strand of her fair hair out of her eyes, Matilda

screwed up her nose and frowned at me as if she couldn't decide whether I could be trusted or not. Then she giggled again and brought her mouth up so close to my ear that it tickled. Even though it was hot and sweaty in the Yu Garden, she gave me goosebumps.

Then she whispered, 'I love Li.'

My heart fell into my sandals. I pulled my ear away from her mouth and said, '*What?*'

'Shhhh,' said Matilda. She looked nervously up the jetty to where our mums were and then whispered again, 'I love Li. Will you ask him if he'll be my boyfriend?'

I said, '*Li?*' And then I stared into the pool and said nothing.

I should explain – Li was my friend. We were in fourth grade together at the Shanghai International First School. He was really good at football and skateboarding and playing the drums and it made me proud because he was *my* best friend. But now here was my *other* best friend Matilda – my *Matilda* friend – standing in front of me and telling me that she loved him.

'Li is a great big stupid doofus,' I said. 'And anyway he doesn't like stupid girls and neither do I.' Then I hurled all my food into the pond. The greedy gobs went wild with joy.

But Matilda looked like she might cry. 'That's not true,' she said. 'Li doesn't hate girls and you don't either. You like *me*, don't you?'

'No,' I said. 'I'm just friends with you because my mum is friends with your mum.'

Matilda went red and I went redder than ever.

My mum looked over and called, 'Hey, what are you two chopsing about?' Then she said, 'Come here, Dylan, you need some more sunscreen on your face. You're going as red as a lobster.'

'No, I'm not,' I shouted back. 'And I don't want any stupid cream.'

'Excuse me,' said Mum, who was already next to me and rummaging through her bag, 'don't talk to me like that and, *yes*, you do.' And to my horror she produced a plastic bottle and started smothering the stuff all over me. Right in front of everyone. Right in front of Matilda.

'Get off,' I said, and jerked my face back from Mum's hands.

'Come on, Dylan,' said Mum quietly so that only I could hear. 'Paid â bod yn boen!'

It was one of those Welsh things she only ever said when we were really getting on her nerves. It meant, *Don't be a pain*.

'I'm not being a pain,' I said.

Mum looked at me. Then she leaned down and whispered in my ear. 'Dylan, we're supposed to be having a nice day out and you've got a face on you like a dropped doughnut. Buck up a bit, please.'

I looked down at the wooden planks below my feet.

How had this happened? How had I gone from feeling so fantastically happy to feeling so fantastically fed up in the space of seconds?

Mum went on. 'Don't do this, Dylan. I don't know what's got into you but it's stopping right now, d'you hear?'

I heard. And still staring down at the wooden planks, I made the tiniest movement with my head to indicate I understood.

Mum sighed. Then, over my head, she said, 'I'm sorry about my son, Matilda. Ninety-nine per cent of the time he's a sweetheart, but there's that occasional one per cent when he's a right puddy-pants.'

I felt my face burn again in horror, but when I looked up Matilda was just looking at my mum confused. And then I remembered that *puddy-pants* would mean nothing to her. It was just another one of those weird Welsh things my mum said.

'Ha,' I said. 'She doesn't know what you're talking about.'

'Well, at least it's cheered you up,' said my mum, and she gave me a wink. Instantly I felt a bit better. Mum smiled and said, 'Is it safe for me to go now? Do you promise to be nice?'

I nodded.

Mum rubbed my cheek with her finger. Then she went back to where Silke and Griff were still throwing food for the carp.

Matilda said, 'I'm sorry, Dylan.'

153

I shrugged. 'What for?'

Matilda shrugged too — both shoulders in perfect symmetry. She reminded me of a dancing puppet I'd once seen. 'I don't like Li more than I like you,' she said.

My eyes dropped to the jetty again. 'It doesn't matter,' I said.

'Doesn't it?'

'No.' I shook my head at high speed.

There was a pause. All I could hear was the splash of the carp in the pool and the squawks of a few Chinese birds and the voices of my mum and Griff and Silke a little way off.

Matilda said, 'So we are friends again?'

'Yes,' I said.

'And you don't hate me?'

I looked up. 'I don't hate you.'

'You promise?'

'I promise.'

My favourite girl in the world smiled and so did I.

Dee's living room was small and way too hot and crowded out by a huge sofa and a huge TV. For someone who liked giving book tokens so much, she didn't seem to have very many books of her own. In fact, I couldn't see any. There weren't any records either, but there were a few CDs in a wire rack which was shaped like a saxophone and, on every surface, there were little brass frogs in a range of different poses. Some were sitting cross-legged on the window ledge and some were relaxing in their own little display cabinet and some others were sitting on a marble mantelpiece with their legs dangling down over the fake-flame fire just as if they were warming their webbed toes. The fake flames were switched on even though it was the middle of summer. The room looked like it didn't have a single speck of dust in it.

'Excuse the mess in here,' said Dee. 'Me and Owen have been clearing out upstairs, haven't we, O?'

Owen – who wasn't very tall but looked like he could lift a truck above his bald head – nodded and said, 'That's right.'

Dee said, 'We've been getting your room all shipshape and tidy.' Then she smiled anxiously over towards Griff and me, who were sitting at one end of the big squashy blue sofa.

'Thanks,' said Griff, metagrobolised.

I just sent out a grateful vibe. It meant the same thing.

For a moment there was silence. Everyone picked up their teacup and had a sip of tea. But not me. No tea for me. I wasn't thirsty.

Alison said, 'This is so very good of you.'

Dee clanged her teacup too fast into her saucer. 'Family is family. And it's no bother. None at all. Is it, O?'

Owen shook his head and looked our way. 'No.' He cleared his throat like he was about to say something deep and meaningful – but then he just ducked his head and had another slurp of his tea.

Alison said, 'And you've met your family liaison officer?'

'Yes,' said Dee. 'Alun. Nice fella.'

Alison nodded. 'He'll be keeping in regular contact – for the next year at least.'

Griff looked at the floor and I cracked my knuckles in the next silence that followed. *Crack. Crack. Crack. Crack.* I couldn't help it. A year sounded like such a long time. Even when time no longer meant much.

Griff shivered.

Dee said, 'Do you want me to turn that fire up a bit, love? You get a lovely glow off that when it's on full whack.'

'I'm all right,' said Griff.

Alison said, 'It's very late – I really ought to be making a move.'

'You can stay here if you like,' said Dee. 'I can make a bed up for you on the sofa.'

Alison said, 'That's very kind but I'm fine. I've got a hotel booked on the seafront.'

'Well, make sure they don't put you on the top floor,' said Dee. Turning to Owen, she said, 'She don't want a top-floor room on the seafront, does she, O?'

'No,' said Owen. 'Uni students living up there, see.'

'That's right,' said Dee. 'And where you got students, you got loud music, empty pizza boxes and poor personal hygiene.'

'I'll make sure they don't give me a room in the rafters,' said Alison.

Griff and I sat in silence as the conversation crawled on for a while longer and then – at last – we all got up and shuffled out into the hallway and went through the whole drama of the goodbye business. But I won't go into the nitty-gritty details of that because I'd switched off anyway. Goodbyes were as common to us now as carp are in the pools of the Yu Garden.

When Alison had gone, we went back into the over-heated little living room. To mine and Griff's and my surprise, a cat was curled up on the sofa. It definitely hadn't been there before. It was black and toffee-coloured and seemed already to be fast asleep. But when we got closer, it lifted its furry face and looked at us.

I braced myself to be hissed and spat at.

But this cat was no Pudders. It looked at us intently with strange orange eyes and then it put its head down again and purred. Something good stirred through the empty space inside me. I sat down next to the cat and slowly reached out two fingers and tickled its ear. The cat kept one careful eye on me but kept on purring.

'You're nice,' I whispered.

Dee looked down at the cat and said, 'I thought I told you to keep out of the way this evening.' Then she gave an apologetic smile and said, 'I hope you don't mind animals.'

Griff kneeled down next to me and tickled the cat's other ear. 'I like animals. What's he called?'

'She's a girl,' said Dee, 'and she's called Bara Brith.'

'She's called *what*?' It was Griff that said it but it could as well have been me.

Dee said, 'You know? *Bara Brith*. Welsh fruit loaf?'

Griff looked as confused as ever.

'I don't think you get Welsh fruit loaf in New York,' I said. 'Or in Barcelona. Or . . . ?' I trailed off. What was the point?

Owen smiled kindly. 'It's a traditional Welsh thing. Goes down nicely with a cup of tea.' He pointed at the cat. 'But anyway, it's black and brown and she looks like a slice of it.'

Griff reached out to tickle the cat's other ear and I moved my hand away. He said, 'I think I might just call her Barry. If that's OK?'

Owen smiled again. He was a nice man. I could tell that already and I was relieved – it would make my job of looking after Griff easier. 'I don't suppose she'll mind,' he said. 'But *I* might. I'm a lifetime supporter of the Seasiders, see, and Barry is the name of one of our biggest rivals.'

Our confusion notched up a level.

'The Seasiders – Aberystwyth Town. Streets ahead of Barry Town these days.' Owen scratched his head and looked hopeful. 'Are you into football?'

Griff shrugged. 'A bit. But only from the telly. I've never been to an actual match. Dad took Dylan a few times when we were in Munich, but he never took me.'

'Only because you were too little,' I said.

'Well, we can easily fix that,' said Owen. 'There's always room for more supporters down at the Park Avenue ground.'

Griff's face lit up a bit. 'I've never been inside a football stadium. We always meant to go and see Barcelona play at the Nou Camp, but we never did.'

Owen scratched his head again. Then he said, 'Well . . . this won't be quite the same as going to see Bayern Munich or Barcelona, but you'll still see some lovely football. We're one of the best sides I've seen.'

Griff's face lit up some more. 'Are Aberystwyth in the Premier League?'

Owen was quiet for a second. Then he said, 'Yes.'

I narrowed my eyes suspiciously. Although I knew nothing about basketball, I knew a bit about soccer. Like Griff, I'd watched it on the telly sometimes. I liked Bayern Munich and Barcelona and the New York Red Bulls and I knew about Chelsea and Arsenal and Manchester United. But I didn't know anything about Aberystwyth Town. I'd never even heard of them.

Dee said, 'Owen, tell him the truth.'

Owen held his hands up in front of him. 'I *am* telling the truth. Aberystwyth *are* in the Premier League . . . *but* . . . it just so happens that it's the *Welsh* Premier League rather than the one stealing all the glory on Sky Sports. It's still top-flight football, mind – in Wales.'

I smiled. This man was clearly an optimist. Griff smiled a bit too.

Owen said, 'So will you join me in the stands and cheer them on then? Well, I say stands but I mean *stand*. We've only got the one.'

Griff nodded and I smiled wider.

Dee said, 'Honestly, Owen. You don't let the dust settle, do you? Five minutes through the door and you're talking about football.'

'It's OK,' said Griff. 'I'd like to go.'

Owen beamed. Then straight away he stopped beaming and looked all serious and cleared his throat. 'Never mind Dee's moaning,' he said. 'There's something you need to hear.'

Griff and I both froze and wondered what was coming.

'We're glad to have you,' said Owen.

I looked at Griff. Despite the fact that he'd been awake for about thirty-seven hours, he looked OK. He looked the best I'd seen him since the drama of the goodbye business with Blessing.

'Thanks,' he said.

Dee said, 'Owen's right. We *are* glad you're here.' She bit her lip and a sad frown fell over her face. It sent a shiver through my soul. 'It's terrible what happened,' she said. 'Absolutely terrible. I still can't take it in. But you're with us now, in Wales. And I really think it's what your mam would have wanted.'

I threw another quick look at Griff. He didn't look quite so OK any more. He looked like he might cry. And maybe it would have been a good thing if he *had* because he was doing such a great job of being heroic that he seemed almost as cold and cut off as I was.

Griff swallowed hard and then he nodded very stiffly and said, 'Thanks.' Just like he had a moment earlier but much quieter.

And because it deserved saying twice, *I* said thanks too. But instead of saying it in English, I used one of the few words of Welsh I'd picked up from my mum. '*Diolch.*'

And in some nearby faraway place, I'm sure she was pleased.

16

Morning arrived with the sound of seagulls. For a moment I couldn't figure out what they were or where I was, but then time and space caught up with me and the living world fell back into its regular position and I fell back into mine. Another universe apart and no real distance away at all, I opened my eyes and remembered. And then I drifted over to the window of the little room I was sharing with Griff and looked out. The rain had stopped but the sky was low and heavy with grey clouds. It wasn't like any July sky I'd ever seen. But that didn't stop it from being there.

Barry the cat rubbed herself against my legs and purred. For a split second I was tempted to pick her up, but then I thought better of it. Careless actions can spook a cat – just the same as they can spook a person. So instead of scooping her up, I only said hello and stroked her head. She twisted her face and licked my hand. The contact and the warmth felt nice in a weirdly remote way – kind of how you feel when you remember good stuff that happened when you were so small that it seems like it happened to someone else.

Griff sat up in his bed and yawned.

'Hi,' I said.

'Oh my God,' said Griff, and froze.

I frowned. 'What's up?'

Griff let out a long breath and then he shook his head and gave a hollow little laugh. 'I'm going nuts,' he muttered. 'I don't even know where I am now.'

'You're in Aberystwyth,' I said.

Barry turned her back on me and sauntered slowly off to get some affection from Griff. I don't really blame her. What was it that Freaky Freda said? Cats only ever really like people who feed them. She'd have more chance of getting food out of Griff than she ever would with me.

'Yes, I know,' said Griff as Barry sprang up onto his bed, 'you don't need to remind me.' He reached out a hand and tickled her head. 'We're in Wales. And you're the cat with the weird Welsh name.'

I put my head on one side and folded my arms. '*Bara Brith*. Not technically any weirder or Welsher than Griff though, is it?'

Griff's fingers continued to tickle the cat but his face was still and serious. Then he said, 'Mind you, I suppose

Dylan is a weird Welsh name too – now I actually stop and think about it.'

'*Diolch*,' I said.

My brother stared into space and let out another long sigh. Then he looked back at the cat and said, 'I must've had more bedrooms than the Hilton Hotel.' I watched as his eyes moved around the room. There was a small desk and a fold-up chair against the far wall, and on another wall was a bookshelf with no books on it. Most interestingly, on a little glass table, there was an old-fashioned stereo system that looked like it belonged in the 1980s. It had one of those turntables on the top so you could play old records. But from the look on Griff's face, I could tell he wasn't madly impressed.

'Give it a chance,' I said. 'Home wasn't built in a day.'

Griff scooped Barry up and hugged her. 'These walls need some posters,' he said.

Even though home didn't get built in that first full day, you have to give Dee and Owen top marks for trying. When Griff and I finally got it together and went downstairs, they were both waiting in the kitchen to welcome us all over again.

'*Croeso*,' said Owen.

'It means welcome,' said Dee. 'Welcome to your first day in Wales. Did you sleep OK?'

Griff nodded. But I just shrugged. Being asleep and

164

being awake were so meaningless to me now that I wasn't sure how to separate them.

'As it's your first day here, Owen's boss has given him the day off work. Hasn't he, O?'

Owen nodded. 'We thought we'd go out for breakfast and show you what *bara brith* is. And while we're about it, we can show you the town. It's *your* town too now, after all.' He rubbed his bald head. 'It's probably not what you're used to, mind. I haven't actually been to New York myself, but I'm guessing Aber's a bit different.'

'A bit,' said Griff.

'You might want to grab a jacket though,' said Dee. 'It's dry at the moment but I'm not sure it'll hold.'

Griff's face reddened. 'Um . . . I . . .' He slapped his arms stiffly against his sides and pulled an embarrassed face.

I bit my lip and cringed with him. 'He hasn't got a jacket,' I said. 'Blessing bought him everything else but . . .' I closed my mouth. I don't even know why I was trying to explain.

'No problem,' said Dee as quick as a flash. 'We'll pick up anything extra you need at Cheapie Charlie's. I work there, see. Get a bit of discount.'

I looked back at Griff and couldn't stop myself from giving him a sneaky grin. I knew what he was thinking. He was thinking about Blessing's sister – the one who worked in the Nike store.

'Thanks,' he said.

I gave him a thumbs up for his manners.

'Come on then. Let's be having you,' said Owen, clapping his hands together. 'I don't know about you, but I'm flipping starving.'

The drive to town only took a few minutes, and as soon as we turned the corner of the cul-de-sac it was clear where we were going. Ahead of us, the narrow road dipped down like a roller coaster and the entire town was spread out in miniature below us. There were little houses clustered together in the flat space at the foot of three hills, and more little houses climbing in all directions up the hillsides. And on the fourth side of the town was nothing but a wall of blue sea.

'You get dolphins around here,' said Owen as we drove down the hill. 'Sometimes.'

Griff sat still in his seat. I'd spotted that he wasn't too keen on cars any more. I wasn't either. It was no wonder really.

'It's supposed to be good luck if you see a dolphin,' said Dee.

'We could do with some of that,' I said.

Griff leaned his head sideways. 'What's that big building by the sea?'

Owen said, 'What? The one *in* the sea? That's the pier.'

'No,' said Griff, 'I mean *next* to the sea. The yellow one

166

with the turrets and stuff. It looks like a castle in a Disney film.'

'Oh.' Owen nodded. 'That's not a castle – that's the old college. But we have got a *real* castle too. It's just a ruin, mind. Can you see it?' He took his hand off the wheel and pointed.

Instead of following his finger, I saw Griff tense up and turn white. I put my hand on his arm for a second and whispered, 'It's OK.'

Griff's fingers fluttered nervously over his seat belt. Then he shifted his gaze towards the distance and said, 'Oh yeah. I see it.'

At the bottom of the hill, the road forked into three different directions and strange unpronounceable signs steered the traffic.

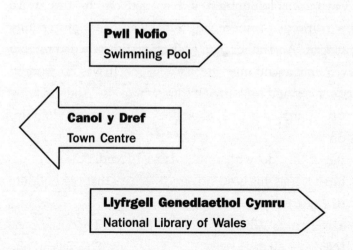

Even with the English translations written underneath, the street signs still looked foreign. They looked as foreign as anything I'd seen on a sign in Shanghai. I looked back at Griff. He was staring at the Welsh words too and looking lost. I think I realised then how very far away we were from any place we knew.

But then I saw that, in one respect, downtown Aber wasn't quite so totally different to downtown Brooklyn after all. The streets were just as choked with cars.

'I tell you what,' said Owen as he came to another stop at another set of traffic lights, 'why don't you hop out and get us a table and I'll park up and come and find you?'

So that's what we did. The car doors opened and Dee and Griff jumped out and I jumped out right behind them. But I seriously doubt that anyone saw me. Because I was so metagrobolised and wigged out by this weird new world that I was feeling as flaky as specks of spiralling dust again. And rather than walk along the crowded narrow pavements and dodge the passing pedestrians, I changed frequencies and took myself somewhere else. And suddenly I was

on
the
top
of
a
hill.

Or was it actually a mountain? It was called Montjuïc and *mont* means mountain so maybe it was. Maybe I was an intrepid adventurer standing on the craggy summit of the perilous Juicy Mountain. But it did look more like a hill. And behind us was an old castle and straight ahead of us was a wide blue sea and immediately down below us was a busy port and the whole of the city of Barcelona. The view was pretty neat. But I wasn't up there enjoying it on my own because I was only eleven. Mum and Dad and Griff were up there with me. And we were all sweating and hot and out of breath.

'We've gone and done it umop apisdn,' I said.

My family frowned at me as if I was an alien. Then Dad looked at Mum and said, 'Have you been teaching them Welsh again?'

Mum shook her head. 'Whatever he just said, it definitely wasn't Welsh.'

I laughed. 'Umop apisdn,' I said again. 'It's upside down *upside down*. And that's what we've just done. We should've come up on that funny little train-thing and walked down. But instead we walked *up* the hill and we're taking the train-thing *down*. That's a totally umop apisdn way of doing things.'

'That's so cool,' said Griff. 'I'm going to start saying that at school. What is it again? *Omop* . . . ?

'Umop apisdn.' I smiled, pleased with myself.

Mum stared at me and a little smile grew on her face.

'You're a poet, you are, Dyl. I named you after a poet and now listen to you! You're playing with words just like you *are* one. You're my own little Dylan Thomas.'

My smile got bigger. It was actually Ibrahim in my class who told me about umop apisdn but there was no reason my mum needed to know that.

Mum winked at me and then she looked at Dad. 'Dylan Thomas speaks sense. Why on earth have we just struggled up this flipping hill in thirty-degree heat when there's a cliff railway?'

Dad took off his cap and wiped his forehead with it. Then he put it back on his head and said, 'For the sense of achievement, my love.'

Mum said, 'I'd feel just as much achievement if we'd come up on the train-thing.' And reaching out her arm, she pinched my dad right on the bum of his shorts.

Griff and me laughed.

'Oi,' said Dad, slapping her hand away. 'Don't you go goosing me – that's sexist! I don't want our sons learning any sexist behaviour from you.'

'Umop apisdn – that's what it is,' said Mum, laughing again.

'You're out of control,' said Dad. 'I should've left you in Shanghai.'

Mum put her head on one side and grinned at him. 'Seriously?'

Dad's annoyance melted. 'Seriously *not*,' he said. And

then he put his arm across my mum's shoulders, pulled her towards him and kissed her.

Me and Griff both let out shouts of protest.

'OK . . . OK . . .' said Dad, and he let his arm drop down. 'You two are hard work.' He grabbed each of us by an arm and pulled us down into a big heap on the grass. 'So what do you think of Barcelona from up here then, boys? Is it better than Shanghai?'

'NO,' shouted Griff.

'Knew you'd say that,' said Dad. 'What about you, Dyl?'

I rolled over onto my stomach, looked out over the city and gave a happy shrug. 'I dunno. It's different, I guess. And it's less dusty. I like that.'

'We *all* like that,' said Mum.

'And it's only a short hop away from Britain if we ever had to go back for any reason,' said Dad.

'Which hopefully we won't,' said Mum.

'And it's only a short hop to Germany if ever we wanted a weekend in Munich,' said Dad. He reached out his hand and ruffled up my hair. 'You could go and see your girlfriend.'

'Matilda's not my girlfriend,' I said crossly. 'I haven't got a girlfriend. I could have a girlfriend if I wanted, but I don't.'

Dad laughed. 'All right,' he said. 'My mistake. But you loved her when you were little. Whenever you two were together you were inseparable. It was quite cute really.'

'Just stop it,' I said. And I plucked a handful of grass and threw it in my dad's face.

'Come on, my red-haired handsome boy,' said Mum, and she took hold of my wrists and pulled me to my feet. 'Let's all cool down and go and find some *helado*.'

'Yum,' I said, and my outrage was forgotten as we all turned our backs on the view and followed the path in search of ice cream.

But just because we weren't looking, didn't mean the beautiful view stopped existing and disappeared. I knew it was still there. And I knew that Matilda was still somewhere too. And saying her name out loud again had put a smile on my lips.

After they were done with the cups of tea and *bara brith*, Dee and Owen walked us around the sights of Aberystwyth. It didn't take long. There was a hilly high street lined with random shops and there was the pier and the ruined castle we'd seen from the car and there was a long sea-front promenade – which was kind of like the one at Coney Island in Brooklyn but without the funfair or the burning sunshine or the pretzel dogs. There were plenty of people around though. And a whole load of them were standing in rows as stiff as rulers and doing some sort of weird tribal dance to a country-music song. From the serious looks on their faces, they weren't exactly enjoying it much.

Griff stopped and stared at them, fascinated. 'What are they doing?'

I stopped too. 'A rain dance?'

'They're line dancing,' said Dee. 'They do it down here every day in the summer. You can join in if you like. Anyone can. See?' Dee nodded her head at an old lady who had taken her place on the end of a row and was clapping her hands as stiffly and as seriously as everyone else and in perfect rhythm. There was nothing unusual about her except that she was in a wheelchair and was being spun around by a girl who was only about my age – or maybe she was actually only as old as Griff. The girl was the only person in the entire dance who was smiling.

Dee said, 'You fancy joining in?'

Griff and me shook our heads quickly.

'Good,' said Owen.

Griff turned away and looked to the end of the bay. 'Oh,' he said. 'Look at that little train! I've seen one of those before. Now where was it?'

I turned and looked too and straight away I saw it – a little train-thing was rising in an almost vertical line and making its way slowly up a steep cliff. The ghost of a smile spread across my face and two faraway worlds moved much closer. 'It was Barcelona,' I said. 'We walked up Montjuïc and ate ice creams and then we took a train the same as that one down to the bottom again. Remember?'

Griff clicked his fingers. 'Barcelona,' he said.

'It's a funicular railway,' said Dee, 'and that's Constitution Hill. Were you wanting to go up?'

I looked at Griff. He was staring at the little train on the cliff and also an immeasurable distance beyond it. After a moment he shook his head. 'It's OK,' he said. 'I'd like to go up some time, but I think – when I do – I'd prefer to walk. It's more of an achievement then, isn't it?'

Dee looked unsure. Then she said, 'Yes, I suppose it is.' Turning to Owen, she gave a little laugh. 'Blimey! He doesn't like line dancing but he's still gonna keep us fit.'

'Good,' said Owen.

'We can always get the train back down again,' I said.

Just as I spoke there was a rumble of thunder and little dark circles began to plop all over the paving stones of the promenade. Umbrellas opened, hoods were pulled up and the small crowd watching the line dancers began drifting away to take cover from the rain.

'I knew it wouldn't hold,' said Dee.

Owen clapped his hand on Griff's shoulder. 'Come on, lad,' he said. 'We can't have you walking around with no waterproof. Not in Wales. Let's go and get you sorted out with something.'

Griff nodded and all four of us followed the herd back to the high street and the shelter of the shops. But behind us, the country music kept on playing and the line dancers kept on dancing. I turned my head for one last look. Unworried by the weather, they were clapping and marching and turning in total synchronicity in the rain. And on the very end of the line, the old lady was sitting under a see-through brolly in her wheelchair and the girl was pushing her backwards and forwards and round and round and looking up into the rain and laughing.

17

Time ticked by.

Late July turned into early August.

Griff put posters on the walls of our room. We had the Beatles on a stripy crosswalk and Kurt Cobain hugging his guitar and smoking a roll-up and Beyoncé looking as sexy as hell in a leather leotard. And in among all of that lot – like a geeky gatecrasher at a cool party – was a black and white postcard of Dylan Thomas.

Not me. The famous one.

And *yes* – me and him had the same name and the same hair, but I couldn't see any other similarities. Dylan the poet was wearing the kind of tragic tank top that I wouldn't be seen dead or alive in and he was staring into the camera lens with the intensity of a deep-sea fish.

'This one's for you, Dyl,' Griff had whispered as he Blu-Tacked the postcard to the wall. 'It's your poet.'

And then I was so weirdly choked that I didn't give a stuff about my namesake's dodgy dress sense or bulging eyes. That postcard was suddenly by far the greatest picture on the wall. So I whispered back, 'Thanks.' Because what else was there to say?

Time ticked by.

Early August turned into mid-August.

On good days, Griff walked up Constitution Hill with me and Owen or stood in the little stand at Park Avenue and pretended to care if the Seasiders scored and pretended to care if they didn't. On good days, Griff offered to do the washing-up or manically tidied our room or went with Dee on the train to Shrewsbury to buy a load more things he hadn't got. And on one very good day, he went to Birmingham and came back with an iPad.

But there were other days when he just sat on his bed and stared at the Beatles and Kurt and Beyoncé and my poet. Or he cuddled Barry the cat and whispered sad things into her ear and cried secret tears into her fur. Or else he sat with that iPad on his lap and wrote long emails to Blessing in Brooklyn, which he never actually sent.

On days like those, I didn't know what to do. Once or twice I thought about properly talking to him – upfront and out loud and brother to brother – just like Freda had said I should. But each time I almost tried, I got scared and chickened out. It felt too weird. And anyway, I was worried about upsetting him and making things a million

177

times worse. So in the end I just shut up and left him to deal with things at his own pace. And time ticked by and I waited.

And mid-August turned into late August.

Dee started talking about the local school. She bought box files and pens and school uniform. It didn't bother me but it obviously bothered Griff. Whenever the subject was mentioned, his face clouded over and his shoulders slumped. One day, he just came right out and said, 'I don't want to go.'

Dee looked startled. 'Oh, Griff,' she said. 'I'm really sorry, love, but you have to.'

I cracked my knuckles in the silence that followed. *Crack. Crack. Crack. Crack.* Then I said, 'She's right. You've got to.'

'Alun's got you a place,' said Dee, who was looking more agonised with every passing second. 'The school is expecting you.'

Alun was the bloke from social services. The family liaison officer. We'd seen him a couple of times. He was nice enough. But sort of forgettable.

Griff looked up desperately. 'Can't I just stay here? Can't you teach me? You're allowed to do that in this country. I heard someone talking about it on TV. What's it called? Home-schooling?'

I shook my head. 'Oh, Griff,' I whispered, 'Mum and Dad would hate that.'

Dee shook her head too. 'Oh, love! You're breaking my heart. I can't *teach* you! What could *I* teach *you*? I'm **useless** with books! And you'd be bored stupid stuck here with me all the time.' Running her hand through her short hair, she shook her head again. 'You need your own space, love. You need to be able to leave this house every morning and do a bit of science and English and maths or whatever it is . . . and you need to have a laugh with some mates and kick a ball about in the yard and pass notes under the desk and cheek the teacher a bit without me ever hearing about it . . . You need your own life.'

Griff didn't say a word. He just sat there with a face like thunder and his shoulders so high that his neck had disappeared.

'I know it's still so *soon*,' said Dee, 'but if you don't start school when term starts, it'll just be harder than ever. And then you'll *never* want to go.'

She was making fair points. I nodded at Dee to show I agreed, but she didn't nod or smile back. She just looked sad.

Griff covered his face with his hands, and when he finally spoke his words were muffled. 'This is so *hard*.'

'I know,' said Dee.

And I knew it too.

I knew it with all the certainty of my soul.

Moving closer to my brother, I did something I wouldn't

normally do. I put my arm right across his shoulders and gave him a little squeeze. 'I'll be right there with you,' I said.

For a moment Griff didn't move a muscle. But then he took his hands away from his face, laced his fingers together and cracked his knuckles. *Crack. Crack. Crack. Crack.*

'You don't want to start doing that,' I said as I let my arm drop down again. 'It's a bad habit.'

Griff folded his arms and tucked his knuckles safely away under his armpits. Then, with a shrug and a sigh, he muttered, 'OK. I'll go.'

Dee let out a long breath and looked at him. There were tears in her eyes. After a few seconds, she said, 'You're the best, you are, kid.'

And she was right again. Spot on. Bullseye. Got it in one.

He *was* the best.

But then again, she was pretty damn spectacular herself – and so was Owen. In fact, the pair of them couldn't have been a single bit nicer. It made me wonder – not for the first time – why Griff and I grew up knowing so few members of our family. Some of them were just dicks, I know. Dad's brother – Uncle Dave – only ever got in touch when he wanted to borrow money. And Mum's parents – our so-called grandparents – cleared off to Australia when Mum was still only sixteen and they took her two little sisters with them. But Mum hadn't wanted to go. She'd wanted to finish her A levels. So they left her behind so she could. Mum slept on the sofa at her best friend's house for more than a year and got three Cs – and that's pretty good, I reckon. And if she'd had her own space, an actual bed and a bit of parental back-up, she might have done even better. Mum never really bothered with her parents after that. And they never bothered with us. After the crash, all they did was send a *with sympathy* card. The dicks.

But you couldn't dump Dee and Owen into any dickish category of family losers. They were top people – and the realisation of this actually made me feel a tiny spark of annoyance at my mum and dad for keeping them from us. But I snuffed that spark out straight away. Bad energy doesn't do anyone any good. Least of all me.

And, anyway, why wreck the atmosphere? I wanted Griff to feel like this place was a place he could stay. I wanted Aberystwyth to work.

Where else would we go otherwise?

Aber was our last hope.

18

Dee stood at the front door and looked out anxiously. 'Now are you *sure* you don't want me to come with you?

'I'm sure,' said Griff.

'He's sure,' I said. 'Who turns up on the first day of school with their mum's cousin? And anyway, he's got me.'

Dee bit her lip and looked pained. Then she nodded. 'Right you are then. Have a good first day. And when you come home, we'll get chips from the chip shop. And curry sauce. And whatever you like.'

'Ta,' said Griff.

'Supersize mine,' I said. Sometimes I'm so flipping witty that it's not even funny.

'Bye then,' said Dee. Then she blew a kiss.

Griff went red and put his head down, but I could still see the little smile on his face.

'She's nice,' I said. 'I don't know about you, but I've

completely forgiven her for the unspendable book tokens.'

Griff put his hand in his bag and pulled out a pair of headphones and an MP3 player. Another gift. He clicked the thing on and put the headphones on his head.

I took the hint. 'Suit yourself.'

We set out in silence and at the end of the cul-de-sac we turned left and began the steep walk away from town and up to the top of the hill. There were only two high schools in Aber. One downtown and one up top. We got the one with the compulsory leg pains.

As we continued our climb, the pavement steadily filled with more and more kids. I looked sideways at Griff and I could literally see the nerves spilling out of him.

'Relax,' I said. But he still had those headphones on. I looked down at the cable which was disappearing into his trouser pocket, and a split second later it was hanging loose and useless.

Whoops.

MP3 connection gone. Cosmic connection momentarily restored.

'It'll be OK,' I said, and placed my hand on his shoulder. 'Just handle it the same as always. Smile at anyone who's not a complete dick and stay a safe distance from anyone who is.'

Griff gave a faraway smile. I shifted my hand and playfully

tugged at a curl of his brown hair. My brother needed a haircut. Even the little patch of head which had recently contained stitches was getting shaggy.

'If this mop gets much longer,' I said, 'you'll look grungy enough to be in Nirvana.' And then – without even thinking about what I was doing – I started singing 'Smells Like Teen Spirit'.

It's a great song, but it was the wrong one to sing to my brother.

Griff flinched and swiped me away like he was swatting a fly. Then he pulled his MP3 player out of his pocket and reconnected the cable.

'I'm an idiot,' I said. And I shook my stupid head and shut up.

Being the new kid in class was pretty much written in my stars. And seeing as how he'd started at as many schools as I had, I guess it was written in Griff's too. But until Aberystwyth, he'd always seemed fairly cool with it. He knew the routine just as well as I did. It went like this:

On Day One, we turned up. We didn't say too much and we tried not to make anyone want to punch us in the head.

Sorted. Hardest part over.

On Day Two we were a bit less new than on Day One.

On Day Three we could find our way to the loo and back without getting lost.

And each day that followed, we'd be less and less new and people *almost* gave up asking us where we were from and which football/basketball/baseball teams we supported and why we had such weird accents. And then – right when we were on the verge of being promoted from new kids to old regulars – either our mum or our dad would get bored and move us to another country.

And then we'd start all over again.

It was as regular as clockwork and almost as easy as eating candy.

But Aberystwyth was hard. And it wasn't the fault of the town or the school or the kids or the teachers – it was just a question of personal circumstances. I guess my brother Griff was totally sick of being new.

When we reached the grey school buildings, we headed for the reception. Alun the family liaison officer had wanted to come with us – just the same as Dee had – but Griff hadn't let him. I don't blame him. Being known as the New Kid is hard enough. The last thing you need to be is the New Kid with the Social Worker. So it was just us. Griff and me. And when all the signing-in was done and a few forms were filled, I stuck close to my brother and followed Meryl the school receptionist down to Griff's new form room. I probably shouldn't have done. I was probably breaking some kind of school rule. But I went anyway because school rules seemed pretty pointless to me now.

'This is it,' said Meryl as she came to a stop outside an orange door with a window in it. 'Room 4a.' She peered through the window. 'Jamie's just taking the register. We'll wait a minute and then I'll give him a knock and get him to come outside.'

First Meryl and now Jamie. I couldn't get used to the first-names thing in this school. In Brooklyn, we had to call all our teachers either *sir* or *ma'am*. Even if one of them was our mum or dad.

Griff put his hand up to his mouth and bit his thumbnail.

Meryl said, 'No need to be nervous, love.'

'I'm not,' said Griff, and snatched his hand away. And then he laced his fingers together and cracked his knuckles. *Crack. Crack. Crack. Crack.*

I shuddered like someone was walking over my grave. 'You've got to stop doing that,' I said. 'Seriously. It gives me the creeps.'

Meryl looked round and smiled. 'I'll give him a knock now – I think he's finished. He's nice, Jamie is. You'll like him.'

Griff sighed.

'Oh, come on, mate – you've got to try,' I said.

The classroom door opened. A tall geeky guy stepped

through it. He had glasses and hair that was redder than mine. I was pleased. Ginger is generally a good sign.

'This is Griff. He's gonna be joining your group,' said Meryl. Then she gave the ginger guy – Jamie – a knowing look. 'Remember?'

Jamie nodded very quickly and stuck out his hand. 'Very pleased to meet you, Griff. I'm Jamie. Any problems – any concerns at all – and you come to me as your first port of call. OK?'

'OK,' said Griff, and, reluctantly, he unknotted his fingers and shook hands with his new form tutor.

'See you later, little bruv,' I said. 'Be good.' And then – without waiting to find out what was supposed to happen next – I turned and quickly walked away up the corridor. Just like I was going somewhere. And each step away from Griff felt like a betrayal. But I could hear Dee's words bouncing off the corridor walls and they were haunting me.

'. . . *you need to have a laugh with some mates and kick a ball about in the yard and pass notes under the desk and cheek the teacher a bit without me ever hearing about it . . . You need your own life.*'

And she was right, so I kept on going.

But I didn't know *where* I was going.

I followed the corridor round to the left and came to a junction. And on the wall there was this sign:

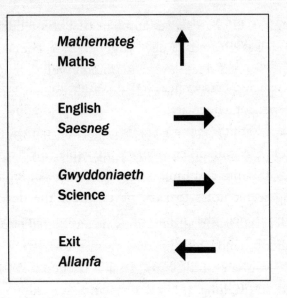

I hesitated, and for a second I actually thought about finding the Year Elevens and doing a bit of maths or English or science or whatever. Maybe I'd even trash a few test tubes and a Liebig condenser while I was about it. But then I smashed that stupid notion right out of the ball park and took a sharp left-hand exit out of the building. And before I knew it, I'd wandered high over the hills that surround Aberystwyth and was back in the nearest faraway place. And this time, it was a

Year
Seven
classroom
in
Barcelona.

And it was one of the very best days of my life. Except that my eleven-year-old self didn't know it yet.

So there I was. Sitting in my registration class. My form teacher, Mrs Lopez, was dunking dough balls into a cup of hot chocolate, and in between popping them into her mouth she was calling out the names in the register. On the other side of my table, my two best friends, Ibrahim and Emilio, were grinning like loons and passing secret notes to each other under the desk. Mrs Lopez reached the name of Rosa Zambrano on the register and then she popped her final dough ball into her mouth. The steam from the hot chocolate had made her glasses steam up.

Rosa Zambrano answered – *Si, señora.*

Mrs Lopez nodded, wiped her glasses on a piece of tissue and stood up. 'Excuse me one moment,' she said. And then she walked over to the door of our classroom, opened it and stood talking to some people who were outside in the corridor.

Ibrahim leaned forward. 'You should see the stuff we're writing here, Dyl. I just taught Emilio the word *schlong.*'

I didn't know what to say to that. Fortunately the classroom door reopened and created a distraction. Mrs Lopez was back in the room and she had someone with her. A girl. My jaw dropped open in shock.

'Matilda,' I whispered. Her long blonde hair had been cut to shoulder length and she looked a bit more grown-up

189

than I remembered but it was definitely, *definitely* her.

Mrs Lopez said, 'Class, may I have your attention for a moment, please? Today we are welcoming a new student into our group. This is Matilda Sommer. She's originally from Germany, but we are lucky enough to have her join us. Now, who can I trust to look after her today?'

Mrs Lopez looked around the room and her eyes swept from right to left and left to right like searchlights. Until, finally, they landed on me. I was sitting up as tall as I could with my arms folded so neatly and so high up that they were practically tucked under my chin. I must have looked like a begging dog.

'Dylan,' said Mrs Lopez, 'can I give this big responsibility to you?'

My arms fell down to my desk and my mouth stretched into a smile so wide that I'm surprised it all fitted on my face. 'Yes,' I said. 'Definitely.' And then I looked at Matilda and waved.

Matilda had a smile on her face that was the total twin of mine. She waved back.

Mrs Lopez nodded and smiled. And then she turned back to Matilda with a wink and said, 'I think you already have a very good friend in this classroom.'

That evening – over chips and curry sauce – Dee said, 'So how was it then?'

'It was OK,' said Griff.

I just shrugged and thought about the maths and the English and the science that I didn't do.

Dee said, 'So your teachers were all right?'

'They were OK,' said Griff.

I just shrugged again.

Dee said, 'So did you make any friends?'

This time, me and Griff *both* shrugged.

Owen dunked a chip into a puddle of sauce the colour of bird-plop. 'Quit giving the third degree, Dee,' he said. 'It's early days. And, anyway, you can't rush these things. You make a bad judgement call on Day One and you might find yourself stuck with a right bunch of dicks.'

Griff and I both spluttered in surprise and approval but Dee just looked at Owen in shock. 'Don't say "*dick*" at the dinner table,' she said. 'Honestly, Owen. Have a sense of occasion, will you?' And then she dunked one of her chips too, popped it into her mouth and slapped her belly. 'I'm as stuffed as a goose, I am,' she said. 'Anyone want my leftovers?'

I didn't. So Griff and Owen divvied her chips up between them. And as I sat there in the middle of this very ordinary scene watching these ordinary people do these ordinary things, I was almost able to kid myself that I fitted in.

19

Matilda and me were
  sitting
  on
  a
  bench
in our schoolyard. It was sunny and warm but not massively so because it was April. I had a hoodie on over my school polo but I could still feel the goosebumps prickling on my arms. Matilda was only wearing short sleeves. Her arms looked smooth and fine and goosebump free.

I said, 'How come you aren't cold?'

Matilda smiled and shook her head. 'It's a lot warmer here than it is in Munich.'

I nodded and said, 'Oh yeah.' And then I tried to remember what Munich was like, but all I could picture was the sandpit at our kindergarten and a fun-park with rides.

Matilda nudged me. 'What are you smiling about?'

'Nothing,' I said. And, crossing my fingers, I asked her the only question that mattered. 'So how long are you here for this time?'

'Three months,' said Matilda. 'The same as Shanghai. My dad is doing some work for his bank again. It's a three-month secondment.'

I nodded wisely even though I had no idea what a secondment was. But I understood *three months*. And in some ways it sounded like a long time. But in other ways it sounded like no time at all. I uncrossed my fingers.

'We can be best friends again,' said Matilda.

'If you like,' I said, trying not to smile my head off.

'I like,' said Matilda – and she laughed that unmistakable tinkly-triangle laugh.

A football spun across the schoolyard and stopped right by my feet. Matilda and I looked up. Ibrahim and Emilio were standing a few metres away and watching us. My heart sinking, I picked the ball up and threw it back to them.

Ibrahim shouted, 'Are you gonna come and have a kickabout?'

I looked at Matilda. Then I looked back at my friends.

'I've got to stay with Matilda,' I said.

Ibrahim said, 'What?' And then, bouncing the ball in front of him, he came closer so he could hear me.

'I've got to stay with Matilda,' I said again. Saying it a second time felt even worse than saying it the first time. It felt like twice the lie. Out of the corner of my eye I could see that Matilda was frowning.

'You don't *have* to stay with me,' she said.

I didn't know what to say to that so I didn't say anything.

Ibrahim said, 'That was yesterday. You don't have to stay with her forever. Come and play footie.'

Emilio said, 'Maybe he wants to sit with his girlfriend.'

'She's not my girlfriend,' I said. 'She's just someone I've known for ages.'

Matilda stood up.

'Wait,' I said. 'Where are you going? I'm supposed to be looking after you.'

'Go and play football,' she said. 'I don't want to be boring to you.'

'You're not,' I said.

But Matilda was already walking away. For a second I thought about running after her, but before my feet had even received the message to move, a group of girls from my class were already welcoming Matilda into their secret girls-only world.

Ibrahim said, 'Now she's gone we can play footie-in-the-middle. You're in the middle.'

Emilio said, 'You should thank us for rescuing you.'

With one eye still on Matilda and one eye on the ball, I stood up. Ibrahim and Emilio moved apart and passed the ball backwards and forwards between them and I played along by sticking my foot out in a half-hearted effort to take the ball from them. And when, at last, I finally *did* win the ball back from them, it took all the self-control I had not to kick the ball as hard as I could at their stupid heads.

September turned into October. One evening, over pasta and Bolognese sauce, Dee said, 'So how was school today then?'

'It was OK,' said Griff.

I sighed and shook my head. It wasn't true and it wasn't OK. Griff was just as shadowy around that school as I was.

Dee said, 'So tell me about the friends you've made.'

'They're OK,' said Griff.

I shook my head again. 'Liar.'

Dee put her fork down. 'I tell you what,' she said, 'I was speaking to Mavis who works with me at Cheapie Charlie's, and she was telling me about how her grandson is in the scouts. He loves it. They go camping and play sports and do all sorts. You could go along with him if you like. They meet on Thursdays. You might enjoy it.'

'Yeah and I might not,' said Griff.

Owen stabbed at a few pasta spirals. 'Leave it, Dee,' he said. 'You're not helping.'

Griff pushed his plate away. 'Can I go upstairs? I'm not hungry.'

Dee looked upset. 'Don't be like that, love,' she said. 'Stay and finish your dinner. I wish I hadn't said anything now.'

But Griff had already left the table and was walking away. For a second I thought about going after him. But what good would it do? My brother seemed to be drifting further and further away into his own secret lonely place, and the only person he ever really spoke to wasn't even a person at all – it was Barry the cat. So I just stayed where I was at the table and watched as Dee and Owen finished their tea in silence. And it took all the self-control I had not to make the sad atmosphere any worse.

20

October turned into November and November turned into December and Christmas came and went. Dee and Owen gave my brother a mountain bike.

'It beats a book token,' I said.

But the bike barely raised a smile and it stayed in the garage.

'Give him time,' said Owen. 'It doesn't always heal but it usually helps.'

So we *did* give Griff time and we waited and we hoped because there was little else we could do.

And as well as that, I started going with Griff to his lessons. Not always. But sometimes. A form period here and an English lesson there. And nobody gave two hoots what I did so I did what I liked.

One morning, while I was gatecrashing Griff's form period, Jamie – the form tutor – dragged an extra chair over to our table and sat down on it. Then, running a hand through his red hair, he said, 'Might I have a word?'

I pointed my finger backwards at myself in surprise. 'Is this about me?'

And at the exact same time, Griff said, 'Is this about my Welsh homework?'

There was a split second of all-round confusion. Then Griff added, 'Because if it is – I can tell you right now that I *haven't* done it because I *can't* do it because I *don't* understand it.' My brother was getting a really fierce attitude.

Jamie sat back in his seat and looked just as worried and as surprised as us. 'No,' he said, and shook his head. 'This isn't about your homework. But if you're struggling with your Welsh, you must let your Welsh teacher know. Actually, I wanted to ask you what you do on Wednesday afternoons.'

I relaxed. So this wasn't about me then. Good.

Griff rolled his eyes and sighed. After a pause that lasted so long it was stretching towards rude, he said, 'Rugby.'

Jamie nodded. 'You enjoy it?'

'No,' said Griff.

Jamie nodded again. 'In that case, you might like to consider ditching the rugby option and joining the gramps.'

Griff frowned. I did too. Griff said, 'Gramps?'

'Yes,' said Jamie, and he pushed his glasses up his nose. 'I thought of it myself and I'm quite proud of it actually.

GRAMPS – picture it written in capital letters. It's the Greeting and Meeting People Scheme. It's been running a few years now and very successful it is too. We've won awards.'

Griff rolled his eyes again and looked so bored that I actually started to feel bad for Jamie.

'Oh, come on, Griff,' I whispered. 'Now you're just being a dick.' And I tried to kick him but I couldn't connect.

Griff said, 'I don't want to greet or meet anyone.'

Jamie gave a quick smile. 'So maybe that's *precisely* why you should.'

Griff frowned and looked towards me.

'No point looking over here,' I said. 'I don't get it either.' Then I snorted out a sad little laugh. 'And let's face it – you don't listen to me anyway.'

Griff turned back to Jamie.

'It's our community volunteering project,' said Jamie. 'Basically, it works like this. We send you out into the community to meet the people who can't easily get out and about to meet *you*.'

I raised my eyebrows and looked at my brother. He was frowning so hard that his face was almost folding in on itself. There was a moment of silence while he mulled things over and then he said, 'But why would I want to do that?'

'For the sense of satisfaction,' said Jamie. 'And for that feeling that you are a vitally important person in this community. Someone who Aber needs. Someone who lonely people look forward to seeing.'

Griff gave him a blank look. But I knew it was just a front. We both knew that loneliness is a very horrible thing.

Jamie leaned forward and lowered his voice. 'And if that doesn't convince you, there's always the small detail that it'll get you out of rugby.'

At last a light switched on behind my brother's eyes.

'I'll think about it,' he said.

Jamie stood up. 'Good. We're having a meeting in here at lunchtime today. It'll give you a chance to chat with the other students on the project. Will you come along?'

'Go on, Griff,' I said. 'You might as well go to the meeting at least.'

'I'll think about it,' said Griff again.

He went.

He had no choice. I made him go.

At lunchtime when the bell had sounded, Griff had put his stuff into his bag and made a beeline for the exit and, for a moment, my entire soul was filled with despair. Because I knew where he was going. He was going down the hill to the pier. And once he was there, I knew he'd change all his lunch money into two pences and feed the lot into those dumb machines that push coins off a ledge. And I knew he'd stay there – just pointlessly dropping coins into a slot – until the arcade attendant threatened to throw him out. And then I knew he'd go and sit in the bandstand until it was safe to go back up the hill to Dee and Owen's. And then Dee would ask him how his day was and he'd lie and say it was OK.

I knew all this because Griff had been doing it for weeks now. Please don't think that I was spying on him. I was just watching over him.

But this time, I decided to interrupt the pattern. So when my brother started walking the wrong way down the corridor, I ran ahead, got through the exit door first and slammed it shut in his face. And then I traced my finger through the raindrops that had fallen on the door's glass window and spelled out one word:

Griff stood very still and stared straight at me through the rainy window. His face had gone completely white.

'Oh flipping heck! I'm sorry if this looks freaky,' I said, shouting at him through the glass. 'I didn't mean to write backwards.' And then I shrugged sadly and said, 'But you're so difficult to talk to, Griff. You're impossible.'

I don't know if he heard me. But something must have registered. Because, all of a sudden, he spun round on his heels and walked quickly back up the corridor. And when I went back through the door and caught up with him, we walked together all the way back to Jamie's classroom.

Griff hesitated outside the door and looked through the window. I did too. Inside I could see Jamie talking to a group of kids. There were about nine or ten of them. A few were Year Nines like Griff but most of them looked a bit older, like me.

'They look like an OK crowd,' I said.

Griff was quiet for a second. Then, very quietly, he said, 'Who's she?'

I frowned and looked at him. And then I followed the direction of his gaze through the glass and straight towards a girl who was sitting at the back of the group, a little way apart from everyone else. The girl was quite nice-looking. She had long brown hair tied into a loose ponytail and she was about my age – or maybe not, maybe she was only as old as Griff. I'm pretty certain I'd never ever clapped eyes on her in my life. And yet I recognised her.

Does that sound weird?

Griff whispered again, 'Who is she?'

Just as he spoke, there was a rumble of thunder from outside and the rain began to pour down harder. We could hear it drumming against the skylights in the corridor. The ghost of an idea started to swim in my mind. But before it could take any proper shape, the door of the classroom suddenly swung open and made me and Griff jump with surprise.

'Good to see you,' said Jamie with a big smile. 'The meeting's nearly over, but better late than never. I was really hoping you'd be here. Come on in.'

We followed him inside and Griff stood awkwardly and looked at the other students in the room. I did too, to be honest.

'Take a seat,' said Jamie. 'We're just sorting ourselves into pairs. We always work in pairs. New volunteers go out with experienced volunteers. It works better that way, see.'

Griff nodded nervously and I started to feel like a real douchebag. I'd basically bullied my brother into this – what with my stupid spooky backwards writing and all.

'Oh, mate, I'm so sorry,' I muttered.

But Griff wasn't listening to me. Instead he was listening very intently to Jamie. And when I tuned back in again and listened myself, Jamie was saying this:

'So, Griff – I'm pairing you up with Harry. There's a

very nice old guy called Powell Roberts who has requested to be part of our scheme. Powell lives in the same sheltered accommodation that Harry visits. So that means you and Harry can go along there together next Wednesday. Just go once and see how you get on and we'll have a chat about it after . . . OK?'

Griff nodded uncertainly.

Jamie said, 'Is that OK with you too, Harry?'

And somewhere – behind us – this Harry kid must have nodded too.

Jamie clapped his hands together. 'OK, so that just about wraps it up. I'll get envelopes out to all of you with your ID badges and some important information. Don't forget to wear those badges and don't forget that you must always report to the care warden or whoever is in charge. Don't just wander into these places willy-nilly, please. The sign-in system is there to keep everyone safe.'

Everyone started to pick up their bags.

'Oh,' added Jamie, 'and, most important of all, don't forget that there is no nicer way you could be spending your Wednesday afternoons. You are all lovely, *lovely* people. *Diolch yn fawr.*'

I saw Griff go a bit red and I knew he was feeling guilty about his lousy motives.

'Just because it gets you out of rugby, it doesn't mean you aren't lovely too,' I said. But Griff wasn't hearing it. He stood up to go.

'Wait a sec, Griff,' said Jamie. 'Don't rush off. Say hi to Harry first.' Jamie waved at Harry, who was somewhere behind us, and then he wandered away to speak to someone else.

Griff shrugged and turned around to meet this Harry kid. We both did.

And there he was. Only he wasn't a guy at all. He was a girl. The same girl we'd spotted earlier with the familiar face.

She waved her hand at him and smiled. 'Yeah, I know,' she said, 'shock horror – Harry is a girl! Only I'm Hari with just one *r* and an *i* instead of two *r*'s and a *y*. And it's not short for Harriet, OK? It's short for Angharad.'

This girl called Hari certainly wasn't shy.

Griff gave her an awkward smile back. Then he said, 'I'm Griff.' He paused and added, 'Also with one *r* and an *i*.'

'Ha! Nice line,' I said, and I clapped my brother on the back.

Griff's face brightened. 'That's *it*,' he said suddenly. 'I know where I've seen you! It was ages ago. You were line dancing on the prom.'

'*Very* nice line,' I said. 'Flipping heck, Griff, I never knew you were so smooth with the women!'

Hari rolled her eyes. 'Oh my God! It wasn't even *me* – it was my old lady, Enid! I was just pushing her! Did you have to mention the line dancing?'

My brother turned purple and looked lost for words.

'Just stay quiet,' I said. 'There's no point saying stuff just for the sake of it.'

But Griff ignored my warning. He said, 'Actually, I've got a cat called Barry – which is like *your* name, isn't it? Except Barry has two *r*'s and ends with a *y*.' Griff's face turned a deeper purple. He cleared his throat and muttered, 'And it begins with a b and . . . and that's not actually her real name anyway.'

I put my hand over my face and cringed.

But Hari started to laugh. 'Thanks for sharing that,' she said. She picked up her bag. 'Look, I'm starving. I'm off to get a baguette before the canteen closes. Do you wanna come?'

Griff looked lost for words again. But then he found one. 'Yeah,' he said. And picking up his own bag, he followed Hari over to the door without a single glance back.

I stood there, rooted to the spot, and watched them disappear together. And then I turned and saw that Jamie had also been watching them. There was a smile on his face and it was the sort of pleased smile that Einstein might have had when he thought up the Theory of Relativity or John Lennon might have had when he wrote 'Imagine' or Dylan Thomas might have had when he wrote anything at all. And all at once, I realised that Jamie was just as much a genius as *any* of them. He'd actually made my brother *talk* to someone. Raising my arm, I waved across the classroom at him and gave a big thumbs up. And then I punched the air and disappeared out of the door too.

That evening, over fish fingers, fries and peas, Dee said, 'So how was school today then?'

'It was OK,' said Griff.

Owen gave Dee a warning look.

Dee said, 'You chat to anyone?'

Griff hesitated – a forkful of peas frozen in mid-air in front of him. Then he said, 'Yeah. I got chatting to a girl called Hari.' And then he smiled and went back to eating his tea.

21

Wednesday came around so fast I think I heard it whizzing towards us over the mountains. And when it arrived, I let each minute of the meaningless morning slip past one by one. Then I went to find Griff. It didn't take long. He was in the canteen cramming the end of a ham-salad baguette into his gob. And when that was all chewed up and swallowed, he brushed the crumbs off his blazer and hurried off to meet Hari.

Hari was waiting in the schoolyard. She was wearing a green parka and she had a bright yellow beanie on her head. It made her stand out from the crowd. In fact, it made her look like a bird swooping and circling in the Yu Garden. As we approached, she waved. Then she said, 'Hey, Griffindor, have you got that envelope that Jay-Z gave you?'

Griff looked confused. 'It's just Griff – not Griffindor. And what's Jay-Z got to do with anything?'

'She means Jamie,' I said.

'I meant Jamie,' she said.

'Oh.' Griff pulled the envelope out of his pocket and waved it in the air.

'Cool,' said Hari. 'And you've got your ID badge?'

'Yeah. Got it.'

Hari hitched her backpack onto her shoulder, folded her arms and grinned. 'Good boy. And have you packed plenty of smiles, your best pair of listening lugs and your loveliest manners?'

She might as well have added a sense of humour to the list. Because Griff was clearly missing one. He frowned and said, 'And who are you? My mum or something?' And then he looked all furious and miserable and stared at the ground.

I tipped back my head and stared up into the sky. This wasn't a good start.

Hari lifted a mittened hand and pushed back her beanie hat. 'Wow,' she said. 'Sorry I spoke! I was just looking out for you because it's your first time and you're in Year Nine and I'm in Year Ten, but in future I won't bother. You're a right puddin'-pants, you are!' And then she turned around and marched off towards the school gates.

Griff stood still and stared after her. I did too. Griff said, '*Puddy-pants?*'

I scratched my head. 'It actually sounded more like *pudding*-pants. But she's got a point.' I touched his arm. 'Don't blow it now though, bruv. Go after her.'

For a moment Griff didn't move. Then he shoved his envelope back into his pocket and dashed after her.

I let another second or two tick by and then *I* dashed after *him*. I probably shouldn't have done, but I didn't exactly have a fat lot else to do.

Hari had already made it through the school gates and was striding ahead with a big bounce in her step and her arms swinging crazily by her sides. It was quite a wacky walk, if I'm honest — it was the kind of walk that would blend in better on the streets of Bed-Stuy where any walk goes. On a quiet hilly street in Aberystwyth, that walk just looked a bit odd. But I liked Hari. And the way she pogoed along the pavement was a nice change from my brother's silent shoe-gazing shuffle.

And to my own silent shuffle too.

Hari turned her head. 'So you're still here?'

'Yeah,' said Griff. 'I'm sorry.' He hesitated a second. 'What was it that you called me back then?'

'Griffindor — like in Harry Potter. Don't they have Harry Potter in America? You *are* American, aren't you? You sort of sound like you are.'

'No, he doesn't,' I said with a snort.

'I'm technically English,' said Griff. 'Well, I'm technically Welsh too actually. But I lived in New York until last summer. And a few other places.'

'Oooh . . . get you, jet-setter,' said Hari. Her arms were still flapping around everywhere. Griff's were flapping about a bit too. I think it was because of the steepness of the hill. It's hard to walk down a hill like that and not lose partial control of your limbs.

'And we *do* have Harry Potter in America,' said Griff. 'But I meant that other thing – *puddy-pants*?'

Hari laughed. 'Yeah, sorry about that. It's a Welsh thing. I got it off my nine.'

Me and Griff looked at her, confused. Griff said, 'Your nine *what*?'

Hari shook her head. 'Flipping heck, I can tell you're part-English. Not *nine. N, a, i, n – nain*. It means nana.'

Griff bit his lip. 'I'm never gonna get the hang of being here.'

'Yes, you will,' I said.

'Yeah, you will, jet-setter,' said Hari. 'You've just got to give it time, haven't you?'

I smiled. It was what we'd all been saying. Me and Angelo and Blessing and Dee and especially Owen. And now this girl with the wacky walk was saying it as well. And, for once, Griff actually seemed to be listening.

Griff said, 'It was just weird hearing you say *puddy-pants* because it was something my mum used to say.'

I looked around at him sharply. He'd gone a bit pink but otherwise he seemed OK. For a few seconds no one spoke and we all kept on walking at a perilous pace down the hill. Hari's arms were still swinging about wildly, but I noticed that some of the bounce had gone out of her step. After a minute or so more, she gave my brother a little sideways glance and said, 'Did she used to call you *sweetie* all the time as well?'

Griff shook his head.

Hari gave him a little smile. 'Well, she should've done, because that's a very Welsh thing to do. And, anyway, you *are* quite sweet when you're not being a total puddin'-pants.' And then she swung her arms harder and stomped off ahead of us down the pavement.

'She definitely likes you,' I said to Griff.

Griff just bit his lip and grinned.

And without even meaning to quit the conversation, I suddenly realised I'd drifted right away from him. And this time, me and Matilda were lying down side by side and

swinging

crazily

in

a

hammock

under

a

perfect blue Barcelona sky. The hammock belonged to Matilda's parents and it was on the terrace of their temporary apartment. It was a much posher apartment and a much bigger terrace than anything I was used to. They even had a pool. I'd never lived anywhere with its own pool. But that's because neither of my parents were high-flying big-shot bankers. Not like Sven the stockbroker.

'This is so cool,' I said. 'You must live in the best apartment in Barcelona. I bet even Lionel Messi's house isn't better than this.'

'Don't be silly,' said Matilda. 'He probably has a much better hammock and he probably has a water slide in his *Schwimmbad*.' She shifted her arm and dug me in the ribs with her elbow. 'Anyway, we are going back to Munich soon, so you better make the most of this while you can.'

I stopped shifting my weight from side to side and just let the hammock swing itself out. Looking up at that perfect sky, I said, 'Do you *want* to go back to Munich?' I had my fingers crossed. I wanted Matilda to say no.

Matilda put her arms behind her head, accidently elbowing me in the ear. 'Yes,' she said.

I sat up. The hammock wobbled dangerously.

'Careful!' she said. 'You'll tip us out.'

I swung my feet over the sides to hold us steady. Then I said, 'Really? You really, *seriously* want to go?'

Matilda squinted at me and nodded. 'Yes. Oma and Opa are in Munich. I miss them.'

I looked at her confused.

'My nana and granddad,' said Matilda.

'Oh.' I nodded and gave a helpless silent shrug. I'd never

missed my own grandparents. I'd never really had them in the first place.

Matilda propped herself up on her elbow and looked at me. Her eyes were twinkling cheekily in a way that I'd seen them do before. *Oh my God*, I thought. *What's she going to say now?*

'Anyway,' she said, 'when I'm gone, you won't have to pretend to hate me at school.'

I jumped up onto my feet. The hammock lurched and I quickly grabbed hold of it to stop Matilda from falling out. When she'd finished shrieking, I said, 'I don't ever pretend to hate you!'

'Yes, you do,' said Matilda. 'All the time! You hardly speak to me. And if Emilio or Ibrahim are around, you won't even look at me. It's funny. I told Mama and she thinks it's sweet.'

I stood there – in my Barcelona T-shirt and football shorts – and stared at her in shock. Then I said, 'You told your mum?'

Matilda giggled and clapped her hand over her mouth. 'Yes. Shall I tell you what she said?'

'No,' I said. I was already looking around for my embarrassingly bad phone – no Internet and strictly for texts only – so I could text my mum and tell her to come and get me.

Matilda said, 'Mama thinks you pretend to hate me at school so that your friends won't guess that you love me.'

214

I put my hands on top of my head in total horror. 'Your mum is wrong,' I said. 'Your mum is being a freak!'

Behind me, there was a cough and a voice said, 'Hello, Dylan.'

I spun round on my bare heels. Matilda's mum, Silke, was standing behind me carrying a tray with two glasses of cola on it. She said, 'Oh dear . . . this is awkward, isn't it?'

'I . . . I didn't mean . . .' I stared at her hopelessly. Sometimes, when you're stuck it's best to just shut up.

'That's a relief,' said Silke. 'If I thought you meant it, I'd have to push you in the pool.'

Matilda giggled.

Silke looked at her and then back at me. 'Has Matilda been annoying you? She can be a terrible girl sometimes. Just ignore her if she is like this.'

Matilda looked outraged. I couldn't stop myself from giving her a little smirk of triumph. Silke put the tray down on a plastic table. Then she looked at me and said, 'So am I forgiven for this wrong freakish thing that I have done? Are we still friends?'

'Yes,' I said, and smiled bigger.

'Good,' said Silke. 'And never mind Matilda – just keep being the same as you are, Dylan. Always.' And she smiled back at me, shook a comedy fist at Matilda and went back indoors.

I kind of wonder how much of our conversation she overheard. I think she might have heard all of it.

Matilda got out of the hammock, picked up one of the glasses of cola and sat down by the edge of the pool, her feet dangling in the water. After a drink, she put down her glass and said, 'So *do* you love me?'

For a second I stared at her, exasperated. Then I just gave up and laughed. 'A little bit,' I said. 'But *really* not much.' And then I did what I should've done earlier and pushed her into the pool.

At the bottom of the hill, we took a left, then a right and then another left and cut across a park until we came to a stop outside a neat block of flats.

'This is it,' said Hari.

Griff and me looked around.

'It doesn't look much like an old people's home,' said Griff.

'It's not,' said Hari. 'It's sheltered accommodation. The oldies who live here have their own flats because they can look after themselves. They just need a warden keeping an eye out for them. Come on – we'll go and meet her now and get signed in. She's called Hev.'

Hev? Or did she say *Heth*?

Griff said, 'She's called *what*?'

Hari rolled her eyes. '*H, e, d, d*. It means peace. It looks like head. It's pronounced *Hevth*.' And she pushed her tongue through her teeth and made that strange sound that was sort of like a *v* and sort of like a *th* but not quite like either. 'It's Welsh, it is,' she helpfully added. Then she pushed the buzzer next to the entrance door of the flats.

The intercom crackled and a woman's voice said something Welsh and unspellable. Then she said, 'Who is it?'

'Hari Parry,' said Hari.

'Oh my God. That is the best name ever,' I said. And Griff smiled again.

'I got the new kid with me – Griff Taylor,' said Hari into the intercom.

'Oh, right you are – come on in, loves. I'm buzzing you now.'

There was a loud buzz and Hari pushed open the door.

Hedd was waiting for us by her own front door, which was just inside the ground-floor hallway. She was like a blonde-headed version of Dee. Small and short-haired and middle-aged and smiley. 'Hiya, loves,' she said. 'Hiya, Griff. So good of you to volunteer – it makes a helluva difference to the residents, you know. Look, it's just a formality but I gotta check your ID card just this first time.'

'Course,' said Griff, and he unzipped his coat so she could see it.

'I'm his brother,' I said – just to be a part of things. 'I promise I won't be any bother.'

'No probs at all,' said Hedd, smiling at the identity

badge. 'That's all lovely. Now, Hari can show you where you're going, because Powell lives in the flat next door to Enid. I've already given them a buzz so they'll have their doors open. Do you want me to come with you this first time, Griff? To introduce you?'

'It's OK,' said Griff.

'There we are then,' said Hedd, 'but if you need me for **anything at all**, just pull the red warden cord. There's one in the kitchen and one in the loo. And Powell's got a buzzer on a lanyard around his neck as well but you're probably best to leave that one alone. OK?'

'OK, ma'am,' said Griff, and instantly went red.

Me and Hari looked at him. 'You're not in New York now, you know,' I said.

And Hari said, '*Ma'am?*'

'Aww . . . aren't you gorgeous,' said Hedd, 'But, please – just call me Hedd.' And there it was again – that difficult *vth* sound.

'OK, ma'am,' said Griff. And he went redder than ever.

When Hedd was back in her flat and we were at the top of the stairs, Griff said, 'I wish she just had an easy name like Griff or . . . or Dee. Welsh is even harder to get my head around than Chinese.'

Hari shrugged. 'But Dee's not a *proper* name, is it?'

'Yes, it is,' said Griff, suddenly offended. 'I know a Dee! She's my . . .' He stopped then – totally lost for words.

'She's your guardian,' I said.

Hari said, 'Your what?'

'It doesn't matter,' said Griff. He nodded at the two open doors on the landing and whispered, 'Come on, let's just get this GRUMPS thing over and done with.' He tapped on the open door that had 'Powell Roberts' written on it on a small cardboard sign.

Hari hesitated. 'You sure you're gonna be all right?'

'No,' said Griff. 'But I can't stand here dicking about all day, can I?' And he knocked again, a little louder.

A voice on the other side of the door shouted, 'Come in, boy.'

'See you in an hour,' said Hari. 'And good luck.'

Griff walked nervously into the flat. I was right behind him. We'd barely gone two steps before an old man appeared. He looked quite fierce and had loads of wavy white hair and was leaning heavily on a walking stick. He said, 'Ha! So you're my company, are you?'

Griff did a double-shouldered shrug. 'I guess so. I'm Griff, by the way.'

'And I'm Dylan,' I said. Just because.

Still leaning on his walking stick, the fierce old man stuck out his free hand. 'I'm Powell,' he said. And then he gave my brother a fierce shake of the hand. 'Come through and I'll make you a cup of tea.' He had a weird accent. I could hear the Welsh in it, definitely – but he sounded Welsh in the same way that Griff and I sounded English. And that was almost – but not quite.

We followed Powell down the hallway and I could tell that Griff was finding each step a struggle. The way he moved you'd think he had lead in his shoes. It made me feel bad again. Maybe this wasn't such a genius idea after all. What on earth were my brother and this old man ever going to talk about for a whole hour?

But when we entered Powell's living room, we both got an immediate and happy surprise. Powell's little living room was full of things. And most of those things were old LP records. Racks and racks of them filled one wall and on the other walls were lots of framed photographs. In one corner there was an old record player in a polished wooden case and in another there was a big boxy television. It was almost like being back in Blessing's house.

'You've got records,' said Griff, and his face lit up like the sun.

'Cool,' I said, and, like a moth drawn to a light bulb, I walked straight over to them to have a look.

Powell's face lit up a bit too. It made him look a lot less fierce. 'So you like records, do you?'

We both nodded.

'Ha,' said Powell. 'And there's me thinking that the young ones today just like all this file-sharing rubbish. Goes to show you never can tell, doesn't it?'

I waggled my finger in front of the racks and traced an invisible line along the spines of the records. Powell

220

had a lot of old stuff − stuff that seemed even older than the Beatles and the Beach Boys − and it was all organised alphabetically, just as it should be. I leaned forward, turned my head sideways and read the names printed in miniature. Frank Sinatra. Matt Monro. Tom Jones. Buddy Holly. *Loads* of Buddy Holly.

Behind me, I heard Griff say, 'You got any Kanye West among that lot?' So maybe my brother *had* packed his sense of humour after all.

Powell said, 'No, but I've got the latest album by Jay-Zed.'

I swung round and looked at Powell in shock. '*Really?*'

Powell placed both hands on his walking stick, tipped back his head and laughed. 'Ha,' he said. 'I was joking!' So *he* had a sense of humour as well. This was shaping up to be a right old laugh.

Griff gave an embarrassed grin. 'OK − but seriously − have you got any Beatles or Beach Boys?'

'Both,' said Powell. 'It wouldn't be a record collection otherwise, would it, boy?'

Griff gave another little grin. 'Not really.' He bit his lip for a moment and I could hear his brain whirring as he tried to think of something else to say.

If you're stuck, keep it shut, I said. Not out loud − just in my head.

But I needn't have worried. My brother was on fire. 'What about Aretha Franklin? She's the Queen of Soul.'

Powell stared hard at my brother. 'I know who she is,

son,' he said. And then he shifted his stick and walked over to his records and stood next to me. I stood aside and watched as he ran his finger along one rack until he came to the *F*s. And then he pulled a record out.

Griff said, 'Is it her 1961 album? If it *is* and it's original, it's worth an absolute *mint*.' I shook my head at him. He was actually showing off now.

Powell said, 'I'm finding you more and more interesting, boy. I'll be honest – I wasn't too optimistic about this set-up. I was half expecting they'd send me some young buffoon with his nose in a phone.' His eyes twinkled and he added, '*My bad*, eh?'

'Goes to show you never can tell,' said Griff. And for the first time in ages, I saw that there was a real twinkle in *his* eye too.

That evening, over savoury mince and baked beans, Dee said, 'Did it go all right today? With the old guy?'

'It was OK,' said Griff.

'And that girl, Hari? She was there too, was she?'

'Mm,' said Griff. He pushed a bit of mince around on his plate and then he said, 'Dee, can I ask you something?'

Dee paused, fork in hand, and looked surprised. Her eyes flicked over to Owen and then back again to Griff. 'Of course you can, love,' she said. But then – before my brother had even got a single word out – she added, 'Is it *personal*?'

Owen rolled his eyes and shoved some baked beans into his mouth.

'Er . . . I suppose it is, yeah,' said Griff.

I raised my eyebrows and sat forward, interested.

Dee put down her fork and wiped her mouth on a paper serviette. 'Look, love,' she said, 'let me make this easy for you. If it's about you being here, I want you to know that we *love* having you here. Don't we, O?'

Owen chewed his beans and nodded.

Griff said, 'Well, actually −'

Dee leaned forward. 'I'm gonna be totally frank with you now, love. Me and Owen haven't got kids of our own, have we? I've got polycystic ovaries and O's sperms aren't swimmers. There we are − it's just how it is. And we've always been happy with it being just the two of us. But then we got told that you needed a home and all that had to change. But don't ever think we don't want you here. Because we do.'

Owen and Griff were both staring at Dee. I don't know who was redder.

Time ticked by and it was louder than bombs.

Griff said, 'Um . . . that's . . . really nice. Thanks. But . . . er . . . actually . . . I was going to ask you about something else.'

Owen shook his head and gave an exasperated little laugh. 'I think I need a beer,' he said. And he got up from the table and went over to the fridge to get one.

Dee picked up a serviette and coughed into it. After clearing her throat, she said, 'What is it you wanted to know, love?'

Griff said, 'Um . . . I was just wondering if Dee is your *actual* name or if it's short for something.'

'Oh.' Dee's face was pretty red too now. Behind her, Owen cracked open a can of beer and the escaping fizz sounded exactly like a frustrated sigh. Suddenly Dee laughed. 'Me and my big mouth,' she said. 'I should listen more, shouldn't I?'

'Yes,' said Owen.

'Sorry,' said Dee. She shrugged at Griff and smiled. 'Since you ask – Dee is short for Doyce-lee. It's a Welsh name.'

At least, it *sounded* like Doyce-lee.

Griff frowned. 'How do you spell that?'

'Exactly as it sounds,' said Dee. '*D, w, y, s, l, i* – Dwysli.'

Griff shook his head and gave a small lost smile. 'I'm never gonna get used to living here.'

'Yes, you will,' said Owen.

'It just takes time,' I said.

Dee smiled her big smile. 'He's right.'

And Griff somehow managed to smile again, even though there were tears in his eyes. 'I know he is,' he said.

22

The next morning, I didn't walk to school with Griff. He
went on his mountain bike. I watched in astonishment as
he wheeled the previously unloved bike out of the garage,
swung his leg over the crossbar and pedalled off without
me.

'Oi,' I shouted as he disappeared around the corner
of the cul-de-sac, '*be careful*.'

I never expected him to hear. Not for one second. But
suddenly there he was again – pedalling back towards me.
He skidded to a halt outside Dee and Owen's house,
dumped the bike down on the driveway and went back
into the garage. And when he came out again a moment
or two later, he was wearing a white skate helmet.

I guess voices can carry a whole lot further than you
think.

'You look like a storm trooper,' I said.

Griff stooped to check himself out in the wing mirror of Owen's car and gave a pleased little nod at his reflection. Then he picked the bike up, got back on it and went racing away again. I chased after him just as far as the end of the close and then I stopped and watched as he struggled on up the hill. He was standing upright on his pedals – his butt high above the seat – and he was attacking that steep slope with every ounce of strength that he had. I shook my head in admiration. It takes proper guts to tackle an uphill climb like that, and my gutsy little brother had guts to spare. I kept my eyes fixed on him until I couldn't see him any more and then I started to walk up the hill alone.

But after a few steps I stopped.

Because I wasn't actually getting anywhere.

It was like riding a bike and feeling your feet spin round at a million miles an hour because the chain has fallen off.

And it was utterly, utterly pointless.

I stood dead still on the pavement and didn't know what to do. Then, very slowly, I turned a full 360 degrees. From every angle, the world looked enormous and grey and empty.

'Come on, Dyl,' I whispered, 'hold it together.'

I closed my eyes, stretched out my arms and turned again. Only this time I turned a little faster. 'Keep positive,' I said. 'Don't get stuck in the moment.'

The bad energy began to leave me.

With my eyes still shut, I turned even faster. 'Time

passes,' I shouted out loud. 'Listen – time passes.' And I kept on turning round and round, faster and faster, until I was sure I was spinning exactly like a column of spiralling dust and then I faded right out of the picture and went

back

to

Barcelona.

And this time I was twelve years old and racing across the beach on a bicycle. Only I wasn't going anywhere fast. A fraction of an inch in front of me, Ibrahim was huffing and puffing and pedalling as hard as he could and his bike was zigzagging crazily along the sand under our double weight. But I didn't care. I was clinging on to his sides and laughing my head off. 'Go faster,' I said, shouting at Ibrahim's back. 'He's beating us.'

'You two are so slow,' shouted Emilio, who was racing along beside us on his own bike. 'You are as slow as a . . .' For a moment words failed him and he just pedalled. But then he turned again, waved a finger at us and shouted in Spanish, '*tortuga!*' And then his front wheel skidded in the sand, his handlebars twisted clean away from him and he and his bicycle crashed down into the sand.

'Ha ha,' I shouted as Ibrahim and I wobbled dangerously past him to the finishing line drawn in the sand. '*Las tortugas ganan!* The tortoises win.'

Ibrahim stopped pedalling and we both fell sideways too. For a second, all three of us lay flat on our backs on the beach. Emilio was making dramatic noises and pretending to be injured, Ibrahim was still huffing and puffing and I was still laughing my head off.

'Seriously,' said Ibrahim, 'you've got to get your own bike, Dyl. You weigh a ton.'

'No, I don't,' I said, still laughing – but also sort of offended.

'It's not a fair race,' said Ibrahim. 'Because whoever gives you a seatie always loses.'

I sat up. 'But we just won,' I said.

'Only because I was riding like a dick,' said Emilio. And even though I was still a bit offended by Ibrahim's remark, I smiled. Because Emilio had just used a word he'd learned from me.

'I mean it though,' said Ibrahim, sitting up too and shoving me in the arm. 'Get your parents to buy you a bike.' Giving me a sly grin, he added, 'You can tell them it's the only thing that can possibly make you happy again now that Matilda has gone back to Munich.'

I kicked Ibrahim hard.

'**Ow**,' he said. 'Touchy.'

I pulled my baseball cap lower over my eyes and frowned. But I wasn't frowning about Matilda – I'd forgotten about her ages ago – I was frowning about my own bikelessness. I'd *never* had one, and it wasn't because I hadn't asked. When we were in Shanghai, everyone had owned a bike and one day I'd asked if *I* could have one too. But Mum had shaken her head and said, 'Why didn't you ask earlier? We're moving to Spain next month. We can't pack a bicycle in your suitcase, can we? It wouldn't fit.'

Then when we got to Spain, I forgot to ask again. Instead I just rode other people's bikes or got given seaties.

I shoved Ibrahim back and stood up. 'All right,' I said. 'I'll go home and ask them now. And when they say yes, I'll race both of you and win.'

So I went straight home and I was **determined** that I was going to ask my parents straight out and I wasn't taking *no* for an answer. But when I got back, my mum and dad were sitting on our balcony and sharing a bottle of wine. Griff was with them too – only he was drinking cola. All three of them seemed to be celebrating something.

'There you are,' said Mum. 'Go and get yourself some fizzy pop, Dyl – we've got something very exciting to tell you.'

'You'll never guess what,' said Griff.

But I wasn't going to get sidetracked. I crossed my fingers behind my back and said, 'Can I have a bike, please? Emilio's got one and Ibrahim's got one and I want one too.'

Mum and Dad looked at each other. Dad lifted up his shades and did a comedy grimace. 'You've had two years to ask for a bike,' he said. 'Why didn't you ask earlier?'

And Mum said, 'Sorry, love. We're moving to New York next month. And there's no way you're riding a bike around those streets!'

23

I took the mountain bike as a hint and stopped going to
school with Griff altogether. But each Wednesday afternoon
I tagged along with him and Hari and walked down the
hill with them into town. It was either that or listen to
the endless ticking of a zillion clocks.

Time still ticked by, whether I was listening or not.

January turned into February and Powell showed us
photos of his family. 'That's my son, Leon,' he said, pointing
to a picture of a middle-aged man surrounded by family
of his own. 'He lives in London now. He's a solicitor. I
don't see him much.' He pointed to another family portrait.
'And that's my daughter, Julia, and her family. They live
in Warsaw, so I see them even less.'

Griff said, 'Warsaw? Where's that?'

'Poland,' said Powell.

'I've never been there,' said Griff. 'But I've been everywhere else.'

Powell just looked at him and smiled.

I leaned forward to look at another photo which was in a frame on the top of a sideboard. It was of a woman a fair bit younger than Powell. She looked like she was in her fifties or maybe even as old as sixty but she wasn't more than that. She had very short grey hair and very blue twinkly eyes.

Powell picked the photo up. 'And this is my wife, Shirley,' he said, 'She's never far away.'

Griff frowned and glanced around the room. 'Where is she now then?'

'In here,' said Powell, pointing at his heart. He kissed his crinkly fingertips and pressed them against the glass in the frame. Then, very carefully, he put the photo down again so that it was in the exact same position as before.

Griff looked uncomfortable and cracked his knuckles. *Crack. Crack. Crack. Crack.*

'Don't do that,' I muttered.

Griff pointed quickly at another photo. 'Is this you?'

Powell and I both turned to look. The picture Griff was looking at was so old that it was black and white and seemed to belong to a completely different era. In fact, it looked like it belonged in a museum. A boy of about six or seven was staring straight out at us. His hair was neatly parted at the side and his mouth was set in a firm little line as if he was trying really hard not to cry.

Powell looked at the photo and sighed. 'Yes,' he said. 'That is the little boy I used to be. But it was a long, long time ago.' Pulling a hankie out of his pocket, he blew his nose noisily. Then he stuffed the hankie away again and said, 'And what about you, boy? Tell me something about *your* family. You're as guarded as Fort Knox, you are. You've told me nothing.'

Griff looked startled for a second. 'I've got a really cute cat called Bara Brith,' he said. 'But mostly I just call her Barry.'

I shook my head and time ticked by.

February turned into March and Powell played us every record Buddy Holly ever made. 'Forget Elvis,' he said. 'Buddy Holly was a genius.'

'Yeah, but so was Kurt Cobain,' said Griff – and straight away his mouth set in a firm little line, pretty much like the boy in the photograph.

So I said, 'Yeah, and so is Kanye West.' Just for kicks.

And Powell shook his head and muttered, 'We'll have to agree to differ on that.'

Time ticked by.

March turned into April, and one Wednesday, on our way to Powell and Enid's, we did a detour to a music shop so that Hari could buy a set of guitar strings. 'I never knew you could play the guitar,' my brother said. He looked genuinely amazed.

'Yeah, well – there's a lot about me you don't know,' said Hari. And then she tucked a stray strand of her hair under the rim of her yellow beanie and added, 'And there's even more about you that *I* don't know. I've known you for months now and you hardly say anything about yourself. Ever. I mean – who exactly are Dee and Owen anyway, and why do you live with them?'

Griff bit his lip and turned a sick shade of green. For a horrible second I thought he might actually puke up on the pavement.

'Flipping heck, Griff,' I said. 'It's not a forbidden subject. Just tell her. Talk about us. Please.'

But Griff only said, 'Can we save this for another time?'

Hari shrugged. 'OK, Mr Mysterious.' And pushing open the door of the little shop, she went in to buy her strings. Phosphor bronze acoustic in custom light. Whatever that means.

When we all trooped outside again, Griff said, 'So how long have you been playing the guitar then?'

'Since I was six,' said Hari. 'Feel my fingertips. They're like *actual* leather.' And she pulled off one of her mittens and held her hand out – palm upwards – so Griff could touch her fingers.

My brother's face turned from sick green to blushing pink. 'It's OK,' he said. 'I believe you.'

233

'Suit yourself,' said Hari, but then she lifted her hand and pressed her fingertips firmly against Griff's cheek. 'See,' she said. 'Like rock-hard leather, aren't they?'

Griff pulled his bright red face away. 'OK, I get your point,' he muttered. But I could tell he was trying hard not to smile. I mean — I might be wrong and everything — but I'm pretty sure no girl had ever laid her hand against my brother's cheek before.

The three of us walked on in silence for a bit. Then Hari said, 'Can *you* play anything?'

'No,' said Griff.

We walked on a bit further. Hari said, 'I could teach you, if you like. The guitar, I mean.'

Griff's head nearly spun off his neck. 'What? *Really?*'

'Yeah, why not?'

'Wow,' said Griff. And this time he smiled easily and openly and I caught a look on his face that I hadn't seen for absolutely ages and it was a look of pure delight.

'Nice one, Hari,' I said. And I was so made up for my little brother that I didn't even care that she couldn't teach me.

Time ticked by.

April turned into May and Griff and Hari pushed Powell and Enid along the promenade in borrowed wheelchairs.

'You should have a race,' I said — just for the sake of something to say.

And Griff tapped Powell on his shoulder and said,

'We should have a race. You and me against Hari and Enid.'

'I was **joking**,' I said, my hands flying up to my head in a cold panic.

But Hari was already shouting, '**On your marks . . . Get set . . . Go!**' And then she and Griff went trotting off at a very gentle pace with Powell and Enid whooping and shrieking in front of them. And I just sat on the sea-wall and laughed. Because it was the slowest race I ever saw. But it was also the sweetest.

Time ticked by.

May turned into June, and one day I didn't go with Griff up to Powell's flat. I don't know why. Maybe it was because he was doing well enough with Powell on his own. So when Hedd the warden buzzed him and Hari into the building, I stayed behind and wandered around the back and into the communal garden. It was a nice garden – not as nice as the Yu Garden obviously – but it was still a pretty nice place to hang out. There was a big grass lawn with dirt borders and in the borders there were plants and flowers, and at the back was an apple tree, and under the apple tree there was a bench. But nobody was sitting on it because it was still only June – and even though June is flipping boiling in Brooklyn and Barcelona and Shanghai, it isn't necessarily all that warm in Aberystwyth. Especially not for old people. But there *was* one lady in the garden. She was wearing wide granny jeans and a quilted jacket and she was cutting the dead heads off the tops of the flowers and collecting them in a wicker basket. I sat down on the bench under the apple tree and watched her for a while. I didn't have anything else I needed to be doing. After quite a bit of time had passed, the lady turned around and smiled at me. It caught me off guard because I hadn't been expecting it.

'Hiya, love,' she said.

I looked at her in surprise. And then I pointed a finger backwards at myself and said, 'Are you talking to me?'

The lady looked left. Then she looked right. Then she looked back at me. 'I don't see anyone else around here, do you?'

'Um . . . no,' I said.

The lady smiled. She had very intense blue eyes and short grey hair. I recognised her from somewhere but I couldn't put my finger on exactly where.

'I know you,' she said.

I pointed backwards at myself again. 'Do you?'

She nodded. 'Yes, I've seen you coming and going. You stand out a mile, love.' She laughed and added, 'You're always wearing shorts no matter what the weather.'

On instinct, I looked down at my clothes. It was true. I was wearing clothes that were much better suited to a sweltering New York summer's day. But then again, I was wearing the exact same clothes I always wear. I looked back at her and frowned. *She* was wearing a quilted jacket – just like it was winter or something. I guess that made us about even in our wrongness.

'You're the boy who's always with Griff,' she said. 'Are you his brother?'

I nodded and frowned and wondered how she knew my brother's name. Did she have some sort of *gift* like Freaky Freda in Bed-Stuy? But then I caught another glimpse of those intense blue eyes and suddenly I understood things perfectly. She wasn't like Freaky Freda at all. If anyone, she was like me and Angelo. 'You're Powell's wife, aren't you?' I said with a smile. 'Of course you are!'

The lady nodded, put down her clippers and her basket and sat down next to me on the bench. 'Of course I am,' she said, 'I'm Shirley. I've seen you coming and going and hanging around in the background but I never did catch your name.'

'I'm Dylan,' I said.

Shirley sat back and smiled. 'Dylan? Like Dylan Thomas?'

'*Exactly* like Dylan Thomas,' I said. 'I was named after him.'

Shirley shut her eyes, and when she spoke again her voice sounded *more* Welsh and more *beautiful* than any other voice I'd ever heard. 'Do *Not* Go Gentle Into That Good Night,' she said. And then she opened her eyes again and asked, 'Do you know that poem?'

I nodded. I knew it very well. It was about death. But

even so, it was probably the most famous thing that Dylan Thomas ever wrote.

'Do Not Go Gentle Into That Good Night,' said Shirley again and then she half smiled and half *hmmph*ed. And after that, she said, 'Speaking of which – shouldn't you be somewhere else?'

I looked down at the ground.

I heard Shirley *hmmph* again and then she patted me on the arm. 'Oh, don't mind me, love. You're not the only one. I'm neither here nor there myself. In fact, I've been hanging around for so long that I'm surprised I haven't become a dodgy tourist attraction.' She gave a hollow little laugh. 'You know the kind of thing I mean – queue up here to see the ghost in the garden.' She gave another little laugh, which sounded even more hollow than the last. 'I bet I sound as batty as a barm cake, don't I?'

I didn't know what a barm cake was, but it didn't matter. I turned my head and gave her a sad smile. 'Maybe to most people,' I said truthfully. 'But not to me.'

Shirley nodded. 'Well, you're not most people, are you, Dylan? Neither am I. We are both in a very unusual situation.'

I didn't really know what to say to that. So instead I just said, 'How come I haven't seen you before?'

Shirley smiled and nodded again, but this time she was nodding at the garden. 'I like it best out here,' she said. 'I was always pottering about in gardens, see. Powell and I only ever had a paved back yard because we lived right in the middle of town. I had plant pots, of course, and hanging baskets – but nothing like this. No trees. No greenery to speak of.' Her smile widened but I noticed a faraway fuzzy look in her blue eyes. And I knew what that look meant. It meant she was right beside me and in some nearby faraway place at the exact same time. I kept quiet and waited for her to continue.

'But that never stopped me giving everyone else a hand,' said Shirley. 'Powell said I was a garden pest. He said people got me in their gardens whether they wanted me or not.' Shirley laced her fingers together and laughed, and even though I had precisely zero interest in gardening, I laughed too. Because it was good to be sitting on that bench with her. And it was good to be actually talking to someone properly for once.

Shirley sighed. 'But I shouldn't really be here.' The faraway look left her eyes and she glanced around the garden and gave a sad little shrug. 'I just can't let go though, Dylan. I *need* to be close by – I need to be keeping an eye on my Powell.'

I dropped my gaze and looked down at the ground. 'I know,' I said.

Shirley patted my arm. 'Course you know, sweetie. You wouldn't be here yourself otherwise, would you? You're watching over Griff and you're treading water just like me.' Then she stood up, took her basket and her garden clippers and went back to snipping the dead heads off the flowers.

I sat still on the bench and didn't move. I *couldn't* move. I was too busy facing a fact I'd been avoiding.

And at some point I realised I was crying. But my tears weren't the salty wet tears I used to cry before the accident – they were ones that would never be wiped away or seen or shared. And everything about all of it was just too sad. Because as much as Shirley snipped and clipped and pottered and pruned, the flowers in the garden were staying exactly the same. Nothing was changing at all. Her wicker basket – which should have been full of dead flowers – was completely empty.

And I knew that as far as the flowers and the garden and the world were concerned, Shirley wasn't even there.

And neither was I.

PART FOUR

-

Always There and Here

24

I need to tell you something difficult.

But difficult is just a word. It doesn't really mean much if you don't know just *how* difficult that difficult is.

So let me make it easier by doing a very difficult thing. I'm going to go back to The Worst Place. And I'll . . .

rewind

and

rewind

and

ᖘniwɘɿ

and make time tick backwards past

Shirley and the garden and

the visits to Powell's flat and

Hari

and the school on the hill and

Dee and Owen

and Bara Brith and arriving in Aberystwyth

and leaving Bed–Stuy and saying goodbye to

Blessing and Marlon

and the room filled with poetry and records and

exit music to a film and walks around the block and

basketball with Kayland and Gregory and Freaky Freda

and badass Pudders and being rescued by

Blessing and Brooklyn brownstones and

the hospital with my brother in it and

Eva and Angelo

– my own genuine angel – and

ambulances rushing to a terrible accident

on the Brooklyn–Queens Expressway.

I can see two boys trapped in the back of a mangled Mini Cooper. The front of the car is so completely trashed that the horrified witnesses braking on the highway are shaking their heads and feeling helpless because they know that there's no way the driver and the front seat passenger can possibly be alive. In the back of the car, one boy has blood on his face and arms and he's crying loudly and out of control. But the older boy next to him looks more or less unharmed. He has barely a scrape or a scratch or a cut on him and he isn't crying. He's just sitting very still in his seat and not making any sound. He isn't doing anything.

The crying boy leans over to his brother and shakes his arm. 'Dylan,' he shouts.

But he doesn't get an answer.

Still crying, he shakes his brother's arm again, but harder and – through his tears – he shouts even louder. 'Dylan!'

But again he gets no answer.

And he never will.

Because even though his brother looks OK, he isn't. A fragment of glass has flown out of the wreckage and embedded itself in the older boy's neck – just a whisker below his right ear. And if only that piece of glass had hit him somewhere else, the boy would probably have been able to turn his head and say, 'It's OK, Griff, I'm right here.' But the glass has made contact with his spinal cord and cut it.

And now he's dead.

And obviously I don't want to be looking at any of this.

Of course I don't.

Because that dead boy is me.

And obviously I never meant to stick around after my clock stopped ticking. But the horror and fear and loneliness in my little brother's eyes pulled some part of me back. So – in a way – I stayed even though I shouldn't have done.

I told you I had something difficult to say. And admitting I'm dead must surely be the most difficult and metagrobolising thing ever.

But

somewhere

in

a

park

in

London

there is a hollow tree. The hollow tree isn't dead. It is always full of life. Little children play hide and seek in it and teenagers squeeze inside for a snog or a smoke. Hundreds of miles away, in a fun-park in Munich, roller coasters thunder along twisting tracks and all the passengers scream with happiness. And, somewhere, a girl called Matilda is going to her classes and hanging out with her friends and getting on with her life. And maybe – just maybe – she sometimes drifts away to some nearby faraway place to think about a boy she once knew called Dylan Thomas Taylor. Meanwhile, on another continent, businessmen are busy doing business deals in the Shanghai Tower, while outside the tower a puppet man is making puppets dance. And in a beautiful garden that was once part of a forbidden city, green and yellow birds are swooping low over ponds filled with giant carp. At the exact same time, in another part of the world, tourists are struggling up the steep paths to Barcelona's Montjuïc and local boys are racing their bikes along the beach. All this is happening in every single second that ticks by.

All this and a million billion gazillion things more.

Because life goes on whether it does for me or not.

And even though I'm dead, this story isn't finished.

25

Time ticked by and July arrived. Almost an entire year had passed since that day when everything changed. And I was sitting in my usual place in the empty space at the table while Griff had his tea with Dee and Owen. Sausage, peas and mash.

'It wasn't a bad season for the Seasiders in the end,' said Owen. 'I'd have liked us to finish top three but fourth isn't bad.'

'They did OK,' said Griff.

Owen put down his fork and shook his head in mock shock. 'Not *they*. We! *We* did OK. You're a Seasider, aren't you?'

Griff stabbed his sausage and shrugged. 'I s'pose so.'

Owen shook his head. 'You *s'pose* so?'

'Leave him alone, O,' said Dee. 'Griff can support whatever football team he wants.'

Owen rolled his eyes. 'I know that. I don't even mind that he calls the cat Barry.' He scooped up a forkful of mash and chuckled. 'Mind you, Barry Town had a stinker this year. Bankruptcy and relegation. You couldn't make it up!'

The doorbell rang. Griff dropped his knife and fork and stood up. 'That'll be Hari,' he said. 'She's a bit early. Is it OK if I let her in?'

'Of course it is, love,' said Dee. 'We can't leave her standing around on the doorstep, can we?'

Griff smiled and went off to get the door and I just stayed where I was. After all, it wasn't as if Hari was calling round to see me.

Owen leaned across the table to Dee. In a whisper, he said, 'So what's the score with Griff and this Hari? I know she's teaching him to play the guitar, but are they an item or what?'

'Don't be daft,' I said. 'Griff's not ready to get loved up with anyone. He's got a protective wall around him that's fifty metres thick.'

'Don't be daft,' whispered Dee. 'Do you honestly think he tells me anything?'

'Fair point,' said Owen. He looked quickly at the door and then whispered again. 'She's older than him, isn't she?'

'Only a year,' whispered Dee.

'That hardly makes her a cougar,' I said.

Griff and Hari appeared in the doorway of the kitchen.

'Hiya, love,' said Dee and Owen – that little bit too loudly.

'Hi,' said Hari.

Griff said, 'Do I have to finish my dinner?'

'Yes, you do,' said Dee. 'But there are more sausages under the grill and mash in the pan if Hari wants some too.'

Hari leaned her guitar against the wall and made her way over to my chair. Quickly I moved so she could sit down without freaking me out. 'Thanks, but I've already eaten,' she said. 'Is it OK if I sit here with you and wait though?'

'Please do,' said Dee. Smearing mash onto a slice of sausage, she said, 'So how's the pupil? It sounded really good the other night – whatever it was I could hear through the ceiling.'

Griff went red and started shovelling the rest of his dinner down really fast. But Hari tucked her hair behind her ears and grinned. 'That must've been when we were playing the start of "Wonderwall". I was teaching him E minor into G into D into A. We're gonna have a go at the chorus tonight.'

Dee looked impressed. 'The Oasis song? *Never!*' Shaking her head in admiration, she added, 'And how clever are *you*, missy, to be able to teach him!'

'I know,' grinned Hari. 'It's insane.'

Owen spluttered over his sausage.

Griff chewed furiously and then pushed his plate away. 'I'm done. Can we go upstairs now?'

'Go on then,' said Dee. 'But put your plate in the dishwasher.'

Griff and Hari jumped to their feet and I did too. Griff cleared away his dinner things and Hari picked up her guitar and then the two of them thumped up the stairs to our room. I mean to *his* room. And even though I wasn't actually invited, I went with them. Because it wasn't like either of them was going to throw me out.

In Griff's bedroom, Barry the cat was curled up on the bed. I sat down next to her with my knees under my chin and my back up against the wall and I tickled her tummy. She opened one eye to check me out and then started purring.

'That cat is so soft,' said Hari, unzipping her guitar case. 'You only have to walk in the room and she starts purring like a maniac.' From the case, she pulled a thin square cardboard envelope. It was an old-fashioned record. A seven-inch single.

I shook my head. 'Flipping heck,' I said. 'Not this rigmarole again! You should do your own homework, Griff.'

Griff bit his lip. 'Are you *sure* you don't mind?'

Hari placed the record on the turntable of our old stereo-system-thing and pushed a few buttons. The turntable started spinning, the plastic arm moved across to the edge of the record and the needle made contact with the black vinyl. There was a pop and a crackle and then the sound of a strumming guitar. They were the same chords that I'd heard Hari teaching Griff the other day – only they sounded loads better on the record. Hari delved into her guitar case again and pulled out a crumpled exercise book. 'Here you are,' she said. 'My Welsh homework book from last year. You may as well just keep it.' She flicked through the pages and sighed. 'If I'm honest though, Griff – I'd rather *help* you with your homework so you could do it yourself.'

'That would take ages,' said Griff. 'And anyway, what's the point? I'm never gonna get the hang of Welsh.' He shrugged. 'And I probably won't be here forever. So I'd rather just copy yours. It gives us more time to play the guitar.'

Hari chucked her book at him. 'Suit yourself. I don't see why you have to listen to "Wonderwall" while you're doing it though.'

Griff sat down at his desk and quickly started copying the Welsh words and sentences from Hari's book. As he wrote, he said, 'Dee and Owen will think we're playing along with the record then, won't they? It would seem a bit suspicious if we were both up here in total silence with the door shut.'

Hari screwed her face up into a big frown. 'Why? We could just be thinking. What's suspicious about that?'

Griff went red and kept writing.

'Wonderwall' kept on playing.

Hari said, 'Ohmigod! Oh yeah – I see what you mean now! Dee and Owen might think we were having sex!'

I clamped my hand over my mouth and tried not to laugh.

My poor brother looked utterly metagrobolised. For a moment, the pen went still in his hand. Then he shook his head and kept writing. Faster than ever. The record kept playing.

Hari giggled. 'In your dreams, Griffindor. In your dreams.'

Griff put down his pen and threw her book back at her. 'In *your* dreams, Harold,' he said. 'Anyway, let's just get that guitar out. I'm not doing any more of this. There's already enough here to make it look like I made an effort.'

Hari sat just in front of me on the edge of the bed. Crossing her legs, she rested her guitar in her lap and began to strum along to the closing chords of the record. But then something caught her eye and she stopped. 'You've got a picture of Dylan,' she said.

The record stopped playing, the needle lifted up and the turntable stopped spinning. Griff looked up at Hari sharply. So did I.

'I didn't know you liked Dylan Thomas,' said Hari, and she nodded at the small black and white postcard stuck to the wall. 'I never noticed that before.'

'Well, it's always been there,' said Griff, a bit rudely.

'See?' said Hari with a grin. 'You might be hopeless at

253

your Welsh homework, but you love Dylan Thomas. That means there's a proper Welshman inside you screaming to be let out.'

Griff looked down at the carpet. And then he laced his fingers together and cracked his knuckles. *Crack. Crack. Crack. Crack.*

Me and Hari cringed.

'Don't do that,' said Hari. 'It's gross.'

But instead of protesting or apologising, Griff said, 'I had a brother called Dylan Thomas. Up until a year ago.'

Hari froze. I did too. Griff was still looking at the carpet. Time ticked by.

Hari hugged her guitar. She said, 'Do you want to talk about him?'

Behind her – so close and so impossibly far away – I pressed my palms together. It was almost as if I were praying. 'Please talk about me, Griff,' I whispered.

Time ticked by.

Griff blew out his cheeks, smiled sadly at Hari and shook his head. 'Not right now,' he said.

Hari nodded. She lifted her right elbow into the air and positioned the fingers of her left hand around the neck of the guitar. 'Come on, then, sweetie,' she said softly. 'Let's nail our "Wonderwall" cover.'

And that's where I left them – practising the sequence of E minor into G into D into A – and I slipped off to the nearest faraway place. And this

time

I

found

myself

in

New York.

Manhattan to be exact. And me and Griff and Mum and Dad were standing at the Top of the Rock. Or, to be *perfectly* exact, we were seventy floors above the city and pressing our noses against the see-through sides of the observation deck of the Rockefeller Center.

'So this is it then,' Dad was saying. 'New York City. Is it how you pictured it?'

'It's like Shanghai,' I said. 'But without the fog.'

'It's awesome,' said Griff.

Mum and Dad laughed. Mum cupped her hand around his ear, pulled his head towards her and kissed him. Then she said, '*Awesome?* Griff Rhys Taylor, we've only been here three days and you already sound like a native New Yorker. You're going to fit in a treat.'

'Cool,' said Griff. 'This is the awesomest place we've ever moved to. I think we should stay here forever.'

'Well, maybe we will,' said Mum. She looked at Dad. 'What do you think, Steve? Is it time to put down roots?'

Dad shrugged. 'You know me, Meg. I'm easy. If you want to stick around, we'll stick around. If not, we won't.'

And then he took his eyes off the spectacular view and kissed our mum right on the mouth.

Me and Griff both pulled faces and howled in protest. A few tourists turned to look and then cringed and turned away again.

'Yuck,' said Griff. He looked down at the city that was spread out beneath us. 'I might be sick on someone's head.'

'It's OK,' said Dad. 'Panic over – we've stopped kissing.' Mum laughed.

And then she caught my eye and smiled. 'It seems right you should live here, Dyl. Even if it's just for a while. Dylan Thomas lived here too, you know. Your poet.'

'I thought he was from Wales,' I said.

'He was,' said Mum. 'It didn't stop him from getting on a plane though, did it?'

'I s'pose not,' I said. And then I put my forehead back against the glass and stared out at the sea of skyscrapers in front of me. 'I hope we stay here forever,' I whispered.

26

Time passed by and the summer holidays loomed ahead. Griff and Hari and I walked down the hill on the last Wednesday of the school term.

'I'll miss Powell,' said Griff. 'I wouldn't know about Buddy Holly if it wasn't for him.'

'Just because school is ending doesn't mean you have to ditch him,' said Hari. 'You can carry on with GRAMPS in Year Ten. I've known Enid for a couple of years now. She's like a surrogate granny. I even went line dancing with her, didn't I?' She pushed the button on a pedestrian crossing and waited for the red man to turn green. 'So long as you always let Hedd know what you're doing, it's fine. The oldies like having visitors.'

My brother pushed his hair out of his eyes. His hair was longer than I'd ever seen it. Despite Owen offering to take him to the barbers, Griff still hadn't had it cut.

And he was getting really tall too. He was way taller than me. He actually looked like a baby rock star. Touching Hari lightly on her elbow, he said, 'What about you? Do I still get to see you even though school is ending?'

I raised my eyebrows in surprise. My baby brother really *was* a smooth operator.

The traffic in front of us came to a halt and the red man turned green. Griff turned red instead and hurried across the road with his head down. But Hari was grinning from ear to ear and I was too. When we all reached the pavement on the other side, she said, 'I hope so, Griffindor. I'm still teaching you the guitar, aren't I? You aren't Buddy Holly yet, you know.'

Griff bit his lip and smiled. 'Cheers, Harold,' he said. Then suddenly he stopped and stared into the window of a small shop by the traffic lights. Lew's Emporium. It was one of those scruffy second-hand places that university students like – the kind that sell a lot of random tat. He must have walked by that shop hundreds of times, but now he was looking in the window in amazement as if he'd only just noticed it was there.

Hari moved by his side. 'What have you seen?'

'*That*,' said Griff, and he reached out and pointed.

The window display was messy. I don't know if it even qualified as a display. There were university textbooks standing upright, piles of CDs with cracked plastic cases, transfers for fake tattoos, little tobacco tins with druggy leaves printed on the lids and ancient Game Boys with equally ancient game cartridges. And in the middle, propped up against a pile of yellowing music magazines, was an old vinyl LP.

'Oh my God,' I said.

'Oh my God,' whispered Griff.

Hari leaned closer. '*20/20*. The Beach Boys.' She stood back. 'I've never heard of it. Is it good then?'

Griff nodded. 'Blessing had it. She's this friend of mine in Brooklyn . . . I mean she was actually my school principal but . . . but . . . anyway . . . it reminds me of her . . . and . . . and I dunno why but it reminds me of my brother and my dad as well. I think they'd have liked it, you see. Maybe my mum would've done too.'

Behind him – impossibly far away and so strangely close – I pressed my palms together. 'Please get that record, Griff,' I whispered.

'I'm buying it,' said Griff.

Hari nodded silently. She looked a bit freaked out. I guess she was starting to understand why my brother struggled to talk about his life before Aberystwyth. 'I'll wait here,' she said. 'The last time I went in that shop, the man who works there – Lew, I'm guessing – said I'd got nice cheekbones. What a perv! I won't ever go in again.'

Griff grinned. 'You *have* got nice cheekbones,' he said.

'Shuddup and get your record,' said Hari.

Griff pushed open the door and went inside.

'He *is* getting better,' I said quietly. To Hari. To nobody. 'He's starting to talk about us again. He's starting to cope with it.'

But Hari wasn't listening. Of course she wasn't. She was staring into the shop and her eyes were filling up with tears. 'Oh, Griff,' she whispered. 'Whatever happened to you was something seriously awful, wasn't it?'

A couple of minutes later, the bell on the shop door jangled and Hari blinked quickly and wiped her eyes on her arm. Griff came out again but he wasn't holding the record. 'I don't believe it,' he said. 'That weirdo inside wouldn't sell it to me! He said I wasn't old enough to appreciate it. What sort of customer service is that?'

'I told you he was nuts,' said Hari.

Griff scowled back at the shop and then he shook his head. '*I* must be nuts as well because I bought something off him anyway. Here. Have this. He had a whole box of them by the counter.' He pushed something into Hari's hand. It was something small and plastic and tear-shaped and just right for plucking the strings of a guitar.

'A plectrum,' said Hari. 'Thanks!' Then she did a double take and said, 'Oh, Griffindor — it's got *I pick you* written on it. How sweet is that! *You* pick *me*?'

'In your dreams, Harold,' said Griff. 'It means that you pick the guitar strings. Pick means the same as pluck, in case you didn't know.'

'I know what it means,' said Hari. She put the plectrum

into her pocket and folded her hands across her heart. 'I'll treasure it forever, puddin'-pants,' she said.

I shook my head and laughed. Griff and Hari were totally into each other. They were in denial but I recognised the signs.

We turned left, then right and then left again and after that we cut across the park until we were at the flats. Hari pressed the buzzer and Hedd let us in. For a moment I half thought of going to see if Shirley was in the garden, but then I decided against it. Being dead is bad enough. I didn't need a dead social life to go with it.

So I went up the stairs with Griff.

Powell was waiting by his door and leaning on his stick. 'You again,' he said. 'I've got the kettle on.'

Griff followed him into the flat and dumped his bag down on the dining table. 'Were you expecting someone else?'

But Powell either didn't hear or didn't answer. He was already in his kitchen rattling teaspoons around.

Griff and I pulled out chairs and sat down, and Griff stretched his arms around an imaginary guitar and began practising his chords. But I was staring down at the table. It was covered in photos – the ones which were usually mounted on the walls or standing on the sideboard. There was a duster too and a squirty bottle of glass cleaner. Powell was obviously having a tidy-up.

Powell came back into the room, pushing an old-fashioned

tea trolley, leaning against it like it was a baby stroller. Griff looked up from his invisible guitar and his face went red. 'Sorry,' he said. 'I should've helped you with those.'

'If I'd wanted help, I would've asked,' said Powell, who seemed to be in a particularly grumpy mood. He took one of the mugs off the trolley and placed it in front of Griff and then he took the other and sat down opposite us at the table. It seemed to me to be the wrong time of year for drinking hot tea. But then again, what did I know?

From among all the stuff on the table, Powell picked out a small book-shaped package. It was badly wrapped in baggy paper that had unseasonal Christmas trees on it. Powell pushed the package across the table to Griff.

Griff's mind was back on his imaginary guitar. I nudged him and said, 'Put that down. He's got you a present.'

Griff dropped his arms in surprise. 'What's this?'

'A little something to show my appreciation,' said Powell, 'for troubling yourself to come and see me all these Wednesday afternoons. You're not much of a talker but . . . there you are . . . I'll miss you anyway. *Diolch yn fawr*, Griff Taylor.'

Griff looked more surprised than ever and then he went red. 'You shouldn't've done,' he said. 'It wasn't any trouble and I was gonna ask you, actually, if I could keep visiting.' He bit his lip and looked embarrassed. 'And anyway, I haven't got *you* anything.'

The grumpiness had left Powell's face and now he

262

looked as surprised as Griff. But he also looked pleased. After a sip of his tea, he smiled and said, 'I'd be delighted if you'd keep dropping by, boy. But have that anyway.' He nodded at the package. 'And I don't need nothing from you in return. You've given up your time to sit and chat with me all these Wednesdays. And you've pushed me around in that horrible wheelchair and you've made me dig out all my Buddy Holly records and you've introduced me to Kanye West. You've given me enough.'

Griff's mouth fell open. '*I* introduced you to Kanye West?'

'Yes,' said Powell. 'Very first day I met you. You asked me if I had any of his records. Well, I'd heard the feller's name before but I'd never sat and listened to his music. So I watched him on the telly when they were showing some of that Glastonbury pop fête. He was a bit full of himself, but he put on a good show.'

Griff was staring at Powell in stunned astonishment. So was I, to be fair.

'You're kidding me,' said Griff. 'I'll have to make you a playlist.'

Powell nodded again at the package. 'Open it up then,' he said.

Griff picked the parcel up, pushed a finger into one of the baggy gaps between the Sellotape and ripped it open. Then he sat back – massively metagrobolised. 'Thanks,' he said. 'A Welsh–English dictionary. Um . . . this is . . . this is great.'

'Don't overdo it,' I muttered.

Powell smiled. 'I thought you could use one,' he said. He leaned forward and put his hand up to his mouth like he was letting out a secret. 'You see, Griff – your friend Hari and my friend Enid chat a lot. And then Enid chats to me. And I happen to know that a certain young man has been having trouble with his Welsh homework.'

I put both hands over my face and laughed.

Griff had turned an actual pinkish purple. 'It's OK,' he said. 'Hari is helping me. But this'll be useful. Thanks.'

Powell dropped his hand and shook his head. 'The way I heard it, she's not helping you so much as she's letting you copy her old homework book. But you've got to *try*, boy. Language is important. It's mixed up with the soul of a place, and knowing even a few words of the local lingo will make you feel more at home.'

My brother was starting to look uncomfortable. 'I lived in China once,' he said. 'I didn't learn to speak any Chinese though.'

Powell leaned forward. 'And did China feel like home?'

Griff shrugged and looked confused. 'I dunno.'

'Well, there you are then,' said Powell.

Griff shifted awkwardly in his seat. I watched him closely. I don't know why but I was starting to get anxious.

'Yeah, but it's all right for you,' Griff said. '*This* is where you belong and you can obviously speak Welsh, but I can't.' My brother's voice was rising. 'I can't even *say* the words on the street signs because they're *so totally unpronounceable.* And I'm actually only here because I've got *nowhere else to go.'*

Time ticked by in total silence.

Griff thumped his elbows down onto the table and buried his head in his hands. I looked at Powell in alarm. Powell was looking at Griff in alarm.

Time ticked by.

Powell cleared his throat noisily. Then he said, 'I'm sorry, son. Perhaps I didn't handle that very well.'

I nudged Griff again. 'For God's sake, Griff, give the old guy a break. He was only trying to be helpful.'

To my relief, I got through to him. Griff lifted his head up and muttered, 'Sorry.'

Powell nodded slowly. Then he stretched out a shaky hand and shuffled through the pictures and frames in front of him. After a few seconds, his fingers came to rest on a small black and white photograph. It was the one that showed him as a serious, unsmiling little boy. 'Griff,' said Powell, very quietly, 'I want you to look at this.'

Griff pushed his palm into his eye, rubbed it furiously and then looked.

Powell gently pushed the photo into Griff's hands. 'That was me,' he said. 'As a little boy. Turn it over.'

Griff looked at Powell. Then he stared down at the picture. And then he flipped it over in his fingers.

'My name is written on the back,' said Powell.

Griff picked the photo up and brought it closer to his nose. In ink that had faded to a faint brown, someone – long ago – had written these words:

Pawel Ciechanowski, 7

Griff frowned and said, 'Pa-wel . . . Ki . . . Si . . . ch . . .' He gave up, shook his head and laid the photo down on the table. 'I don't get it. You're Powell Roberts.'

Powell nodded and picked the photograph up. He looked at it, and for a moment I thought he was actually crying. But then he smiled and seemed completely OK. I think his eyes were just a bit watery – in the way that old people's eyes *do* get watery sometimes. 'I *am* Powell Roberts,' he said to Griff, 'but I used to be Pawel Ciechanowski.'

I looked at the old man, astonished. The sound that had just came from his lips seemed to have little connection to the letters written on the back of the photo.

Pa-vel Shek-a-novskee

It was the Dwysli/Doyce-lee thing all over again.

'Back then, I was a little boy from Poland. So I suppose

266

that makes me a bit like you. When I first came to Wales, I thought it was a very strange and faraway place and I was very lonely.'

Griff and I were staring at Powell – or Pawel – in silence. I don't think Griff was even breathing. I know I wasn't.

'That picture was taken a few days before I left home,' said Powell. 'My mama wrote my name on the back of it and my age – seven. And I'm not smiling because I'm not happy. I know I'm going to be sent a long way away to live with new people.'

Griff reached out and, to my total surprise, he took hold of the old man's hand. Then he asked the question that I wanted to ask. 'Why?'

Powell laid his other hand on top of the hand-pile and shook his head sadly. 'When I was a little lad, there were terrible things going on. Terrible things. The whole world was on the brink of war, and Poland was having it particularly tough.' He shook his head again and shrugged both shoulders. 'You think I'm Welsh, but once upon a time I was Polish. And when that photo was taken, Poland was not a safe place.'

Griff and I stared at him. However many school curriculums you start and never finish, you still learn about war.

Griff said, 'So . . . so . . .' His voice trailed away.

'*So*,' said Powell, 'I'm telling you all this because I'm

like *you*. I came to Wales from a far-off land and I thought I'd never get used to it. I thought it would *never* be my home and I thought I was just passing the days in this strange foreign country until it was time to move again.' He tapped the dictionary. 'But you know what? Once I stopped acting like an outsider and embraced the place a bit, it embraced me back.'

'OK,' said Griff. 'OK, I get that. I'll do my Welsh homework – but . . . but that's not what I meant.'

Powell frowned. 'Isn't it?'

'No,' said Griff. 'I meant . . . what happened? When the photo was taken.'

Powell sighed. 'I was very lucky,' he said. 'And I was also my parents' only child. They didn't have enough money for all three of us to leave, but they were determined to get me out of the country before it was too late.'

Griff looked confused. 'So . . . so . . . are you Jewish?

'No,' said Powell. 'Just Polish.' He was quiet for a moment and the only sound was the ticking of a big clock on his sideboard. But then he took a big breath and carried on with his story. 'My mother had a cousin who had married an English sailor and moved with him to England. At least, my mother *thought* it was England. But it turned out that the sailor was Welsh and the married cousin lived in Cardiff. Mama wrote to her – my aunty Dora I called her – and Dora wrote back saying Mama should send Pawel over by ship and she would meet him and look after him until it was safe for him to return home again. So that's what happened.'

Griff had taken his hand away from Powell's and was now pressing his palms flat together. Almost as if he were praying. 'But . . . but you're still here,' he whispered.

Powell pushed his own palms down against the table, rose from his chair and looked around for his walking stick. 'That's right,' he said. 'I stayed with Aunty Dora and Uncle John and, eventually, they adopted me and I took their surname – Roberts. Nobody could spell mine anyway. And Pawel became Powell – just because that was easier too.' He spotted his stick against the wall, took hold of it and walked slowly off into his kitchen.

Griff jumped up and followed him and I jumped up and followed Griff. Griff said, 'But what about your mum and dad?'

Powell was boiling the kettle again. Without turning round, he put the kettle down and lowered his head so that all we could see was his neck. 'I never saw them again,' he said.

For a second, my brother stood completely still in the doorway of the kitchen. It was like he was a freeze-frame from a movie or something. But then the motion returned, his legs buckled beneath him and he sort of slid down the side of the door frame.

'Griff,' I shouted, and I tried to catch him but he fell straight through my open non-existent arms. I put my non-existent hands on my non-existent head and felt utterly useless and desperate.

Powell spun round, grabbed his stick and quickly hobbled over. Carefully, using his stick as a sort of fireman's pole, he edged his way down it until he was on his knees and then he rested his hand on my brother's shoulder. Griff was crying. Massively and hugely and uncontrollably. It was the sort of crying that starts in the pit of your stomach and forces its way out like a volcano erupting. I'd only ever seen him cry like that once before. And that was that time when I died.

'Hey,' said Powell. 'Hey, hey, boy? What's all this? I'm OK. It was a very long time ago.'

But Griff just kept crying.

Powell stared at him and I saw something flicker across his face – sadness, definitely, but there was something else too. I think it was understanding. The clock ticked on and then the old man wrapped his arms around my sobbing brother and held him in a hug. 'Let it all out,' he said gently. 'Whatever it is, just let it out.'

27

All you have to do to make yourself feel better is think of something happy.

And the first thing that came into my head was an image of

me

and

my

mum

in

the little kitchen in our Brooklyn apartment. The kitchen was so small that the two of us were crowding it out. I was sitting up on the worktop, and instead of looking happy, I looked very fed up. My mum was standing by the stove, waiting for a pan of water to boil. 'I'll never understand why Americans don't do kettles,' she said with a shake of her head. Then she looked over her shoulder at me. 'What's the matter with you, puddy-pants?'

'Don't call me that,' I said.

'Sorry,' said Mum. 'I'll start again. What's the matter with you, Dylan darling?'

I sighed noisily and swung my legs. Then I said, 'It's Lester.' Lester was a boy in my class. He was my friend, I guess. But only if friends are also people you occasionally want to punch in the head.

'I thought he was your friend,' said Mum. 'What's he done?'

'He's having a big birthday party,' I said.

My mum frowned at her pan of non-boiling water. Then she frowned at me. 'And he's not invited you?'

'No,' I said. 'He has.'

My mum frowned again. 'What do you mean – no, he has? *Yes*, he has, or *no*, he hasn't?'

I rolled my eyes. 'No – I mean, he has invited me.'

Mum shrugged. 'So why the rancid face?'

I sighed again. Louder than the last time. 'It's his birthday *tomorrow*. But guess when he's having his stupid party?'

'Dunno,' said Mum. 'I hate guessing games. We could be here till I've gone through the whole flipping calendar.'

'The weekend after next,' I said. 'On *my* birthday.'

Bubbles started rising in the pan of water. Mum stared at them and then she scratched her head. 'Well, that doesn't sound too bad to me. Me and your dad were gonna take you out for a posh burger, but we can do that another day.' She nudged the gas up a bit. 'And Lester's invited you, so there isn't really a problem. All your friends will be there with you and it doesn't change the fact that it's your birthday, does it?'

I stared at her in frustration. Then I said, 'Yeah but it'll be *my* fifteenth birthday and *Lester's* party.'

The bubbles were going ballistic in the pan now. Mum turned the gas off and took two mugs from a mug tree. 'Don't go then,' she said.

'What?' I stared at her in amazement. Didn't she understand *anything*? 'Of course I'm gonna go,' I said. 'Everybody else is.'

Mum threw two teabags into the mugs and poured the steamy water over them. 'So stop your fussing and make sure you have a nice time.' From its home on the window ledge, my mum's phone rang. 'Hang on,' she said to me.

I sat where I was on the counter. Just swinging my legs and feeling furious. And then Mum spoke into the phone and I stopped feeling furious.

'Silke! Hi, how are you? [Long pause] No way! When? [Short pause] Oh, that's great! [Another short pause] Yeah, we'll be here. [Long pause] Yes, yes – definitely! [Short pause] OK . . . OK – yes, definitely! Well, we'll see you then! Bye.'

My mum put the phone back on the window ledge

and looked at me with a big excited smile. 'Guess who that was?'

'Silke Sommer,' I said, smiling. 'One hundred per cent. Final answer.'

'I *know*,' said Mum. 'Haven't seen her in absolutely ages! They've booked themselves a flashy New York shopping break and wondered if we could meet up with them for a meal.' Her hand suddenly flew up to her mouth. '*Oh, shin splints!*'

'What?' I said. Worried.

'It's your birthday, isn't it?' She bit her lip and looked apologetic. 'Oh God, I'm sorry, Dyl. She caught me on the hop. Do you mind?'

I frowned. As excited as I was to see Matilda again, I wasn't that ecstatic about missing out on Lester's party – even if he *was* stealing my day. I tipped my head back and looked at the ceiling. 'Aw, Mum,' I said, 'does this mean my fifteenth birthday is now gonna be spent in some boring Manhattan restaurant listening to boring Sven drone on about boring bank things while everyone at school is gonna be at a house party around at Lester's?'

Mum looked at me. And then she shook her head. 'No,' she said. 'It doesn't mean that. It means we'll ask Silke and Sven over *here* for the evening, and *you* can take Matilda with you to Lester's party.' She shrugged and added, 'If she *wants* to go, of course, and if Silke and Sven are OK with that and if it's also all right by you . . . ?'

I felt the corners of my mouth twitch. And then a smile spread all over my face and all over my body and all over my soul.

I shrugged back. 'Yeah – that's cool,' I said.

28

Griff couldn't stop crying and Powell knelt on his kitchen floor for so long that his legs went stiff. In the end, he pulled out the emergency buzzer that he wore on a cord around his neck and pressed it.

Within seconds, Hedd came to rescue them both. She winched the pair of them off the floor, settled them into matching monster-sized armchairs and gave each of them a cup of tea. Then – because Griff was still crying – she went next door to Enid's flat and got Hari. And Griff got better then. He was still leaking out a few tears from the sides of his eyes, but the worst of the tidal wave had passed. Soon he was looking blotchy and embarrassed and desperate to leave.

'You take it easy, love,' Hedd had said to him anxiously. 'It's not a usual thing, is it – crying the weight of the world off your shoulders like that.' And Griff had rubbed his nose and shaken his head. Because she was right – it wasn't a usual thing. But sometimes it has to be done. And that moment and the room and the cosmos and my soul all felt a fair bit better because of it.

'Come on, Griffindor,' said Hari. 'Let's go outside and get us some sunshine.'

'Don't forget your school bag, boy,' said Powell.

'Oh yeah,' said Griff, 'and my Welsh dictionary.' He sniffed and gave the old man an awkward little smile.

Powell pushed the dictionary into my brother's hands and looked at him with watery, pale eyes. 'You'll come back then?'

'Definitely,' said Griff. And in spite of the softness with which he said it, it was as definite as any *definitely* I ever heard. Griff sniffed again. 'Thanks, Powell,' he said. 'I'm sorry if I freaked you out.'

Powell reached out a hand and touched my brother on the arm. 'Don't say sorry,' he said. 'It can be damn difficult to cry. Sometimes it's easier to cry for other people than it is for yourself.'

Griff looked back into the old man's eyes and nodded. 'You're so right.'

'And so I *should* be,' said Powell. 'I'm old enough to know better.'

Sitting on a bench and staring at the sea, Griff told Hari everything. It was a brief kind of everything but it was enough. Some stories you pimp up with adjectives and wow words and a flashy splash of poetic licence and other stories you don't. You just don't.

When all the words were spoken, Griff lifted his Nikes up onto the seat and sat with his knees up around his ears like a locust. Next to him, Hari sat stock-still for a whole minute or more. And then she too shifted her feet up onto the bench and the pair of them sat, chins on knees, staring straight ahead.

'Shit,' said Hari eventually. And then, shaking her head, she said, 'I guessed something awful had happened back in America . . . but . . . but . . . oh my God, Griff . . . I'm so sorry.'

Griff shook his head too. 'No . . . it's . . . it's . . .' He took a deep breath. 'Can we just sit here for a while longer and not . . . just not say anything?'

Hari nodded.

Above them, seagulls swooped and circled, shrieking at each other with their weird seagull voices. From way behind in the busy little streets of the town centre, the distant drone of traffic droned on endlessly. To the left and right, ancient voices of ancient people echoed forever around the scattered castle ruins. And out ahead – wide open and endless – the sea hushed everything and sparkled like a billion blue sapphires under the summer sun.

A while longer passed.

'My brother could've been a poet,' said Griff, 'just like Dylan Thomas.' A smile appeared on Griff's face. 'Dyl was good with words. I know he'd have had something stylish to say about this place.' His smile grew. 'And my mum would've liked it here too – sitting on this bench, I mean. Of course she would. She was proper Welsh – same as you.' Griff turned his head so he was looking at Hari. 'She was so cool, my mum. She had a little silver stud in her nose and she was always laughing. My dad was cool too. They were the coolest parents I ever could have had.'

'They sound amazing,' said Hari.

Griff didn't say anything. He just nodded.

Hari hugged her legs. 'I can't imagine how you must feel,' she said quietly. 'But at least you'll always have that love for them. At least you'll always know how much they loved you.'

'I know,' said Griff, and nodded again.

A gust of wind blew their hair across their faces. Hari shifted sideways on the seat and pulled a scrunchie from the pocket of her school blazer. As she tied her hair back in a ponytail, something on the back of the seat caught her eye. It was a little metal plaque.

**In Loving Memory of
John and Didi Morgan.
'Love Conquers All.'**

Hari read it aloud and touched the plaque gently with her fingertips. 'See. What did I just say? Love'll get you through anything.' She put her head on one side. 'It's nice that someone put this bench here for John and Didi. It sort of means they're still here, doesn't it? Because everyone who ever sits here will read their names and wonder what their story was.'

Griff brushed his hair out of his eyes. 'People you love don't ever really go away,' he said. 'All that energy has to go somewhere.' He went red and stared down at his trainers for a moment. And then he breathed deeply and stared out to sea again. 'It's the Law of Physics, I suppose.'

And even though I knew he wasn't talking to me, I answered anyway. I'd been staying out of it, trying to give Griff some space, but now I couldn't stop myself from shouting out loud. 'You've got it!' I said, and I punched the air in excitement and relief. 'I'm here, Griff!'

Griff rubbed the corner of his eye and kept staring out to sea. 'I think about them all the time,' he said. 'Honestly I do. All the time. Especially Dylan. I ask myself what he'd think about certain stuff and what he'd say in certain situations and . . . I know it's not much . . . but, in a way, it keeps him with me.'

The wind blew again, and on the promenade flags flapped noisily on the top of tall white poles. Even though the sun was bright, Griff shivered.

'It's blowing hot and cold,' said Hari. 'It's always like that here. You get used to it.'

Griff suddenly sat forward, shielded his eyes with one hand and stared hard at the sea. 'I can see things in the water,' he said. 'Look.'

Hari sat forward too. Then she said, 'Oh my God! Dolphins!'

And there were as well. Three, four . . . five dolphins – maybe even more – were jumping out of the sea and swimming together in circles and rolling around on the surf and playing.

'That's lucky, that is,' said Griff. 'I remember either Dee or Owen saying it.'

Hari's face – which had already lit up at the sight of the dolphins – suddenly lit up even more. 'You wanna know what's *really* lucky? You should kick the bar.'

Griff frowned and pushed more hair out of his face. 'You *what*?'

'It's an Aberystwyth tradition,' said Hari. 'You walk the whole length of the prom until you can't go no further and then you kick the lowest bar of the railings. Everyone does it. It brings good luck. That's why everyone who lives here is happy.' She shrugged. 'Well, not *everyone*. Probably not that pervert Lew in Lew's Emporium – but *most* people.'

Griff stood up. 'Let's do it now,' he said. 'Let's go and kick the hell out of the bar.'

281

Without waiting a single second, Hari sprang up and started running off through the castle ruins. 'Come on then, Griffindor,' she said, shouting back over her shoulder. 'Last one there is a puddin'-pants.'

29

I leaned against the ancient stones of the castle ruins and watched my brother and his friend race away down the prom. And then, when they rounded a bend and were gone, I wandered back to John and Didi Morgan's bench and sank down on it once more. Reaching out with the ghost of a hand, I touched the wooden seat ever so lightly. For Griff, it had changed. For him, the bench now stood for something significant. It was a stepping stone on his way back from super-massive grief. But for me there were no stepping stones and there was zero chance of any change either. I looked around. Seagulls were still screeching in the sky above. Dolphins were still poking their noses out of the water and, every now and then, people passed by and looked right through me. Mums with their tiny children. Old-age pensioners out for a stroll. People walking their dogs. Sometimes the dogs turned their heads and sniffed the air that separated us, but they were the only ones that noticed I was there. I never felt so alone in my life.

'Love conquers all,' I whispered. To nobody. To myself. And there must have been some magic in those words. Because, straight away, just as if I'd said *abracadabra* and shaken pixie dust out of my fingertips, the situation didn't seem quite so bleak. I mean, I was still dead and all – there was no getting over that – but whoever put that plaque on John and Didi's bench was on to something – love can cross a lot of boundaries. Even life and death. And before I knew it, time and space had shifted and carried me off to somewhere else. And this time I was

sitting

on

the

stairs

in Lester Disario's house. His birthday party. *My* actual birthday. And one very significant step.

Kids from my school were holed up in rooms and hallways like woodworm, and Kanye West's voice was bouncing off all the walls. The only halfway peaceful place in the entire building was on the stairs and that's where I was. Mid-flight. Neither up nor down nor here nor there. And, to be honest, I was finding every single thing about being fifteen a bit difficult to take in. And I suppose that was partly because of the warm beer I was drinking and partly because I wasn't alone on my step. Matilda

Sommer was sitting right next to me. She'd gotten older all over again and her hair was shorter than I'd ever seen it before, but she was still the Matilda I'd known since pretty much forever and we were sharing a step. And that would have been utterly amazing if my head hadn't been so bamboozled by a great big *IF*.

IF I gave Matilda a sign of how much I truly loved her, would she drop me like a sack of sick or would she show me that she felt the same way back?

It was a torturous question.

So I played it safe and kept my signs to myself. And for ages we just sat there, sipping our hideous beer and listening to Kanye West. But then – just for the sake of something to say – I nodded at my party cup and yelled, 'This tastes like bog water. Shall I see if I can find us some soda or something?'

I had to yell. Kanye West doesn't do quiet.

'No,' Matilda shouted back. 'I *like* the bog water.' She took a swig from her own party cup and laughed. 'My friends in Munich will think it's so cool that I got to go to an American birthday party.'

My heart lifted a little. She was having a good time. Maybe this was a sign? From the floor half below us, Kanye West started rapping even louder. I put my mouth close to Matilda's ear. 'You don't mind, then? Being here with me?'

Matilda turned her face and our noses almost collided. Quickly I jerked my head back, my face burning, and turned so I was staring straight ahead. Matilda put her lips so close to my ear that I could feel her breath. 'No,' she said. 'I thought it would be fun.' My heart jumped again. She took another swig of that horrible beer and rolled her eyes. 'But don't you think it is boring, no? That your dad is coming to get us at half past ten? *Half past ten!* Who leaves a party so early as this?'

I bit my lip and smiled at her. 'Yeah, I'm sorry about that. He's very protective.'

Matilda frowned and cupped her hand to her ear. 'What?'

'He's pro-tec-tive,' I shouted.

Matilda frowned harder and then she stared down into her bog water for what felt like ages. Finally, she brought her mouth back to my ear and shouted, 'What? Of me? Because I'm a girl?'

I shook my head quickly and *I* frowned too. *Was she dissing my dad?* I gave her a stroppy nudge with my elbow. 'No,' I said. 'He's protective of *me*. Because I'm his son. There are some right lunatics around after dark and he just wants to be sure I get home safe. But now you come to mention it, I'm sure he'd feel happier if *you* got home safe too.'

I got a stroppy nudge back. 'This party is boring anyway,' shouted Matilda.

My heart bombed. She was bored. *Bored?* I could have sat with her in the middle of the Mojave Desert and not been bored.

Kanye West suddenly calmed down. I think either Lester's mum or dad had pushed their way through to the laptop or iPod or stereo or whatever. I was glad. It meant we could stop shrieking at each other. Matilda tipped her wrist and looked at her watch. Some of the bad beer spilled out onto the carpet. 'We've only got thirty-three minutes left until your dad comes,' she said, and puffed out her cheeks in the most bored way ever. 'I've sat on this step with you all evening and talked about nothing.'

I stared down at my trainers uncomfortably. My fifteenth birthday was shaping up to be a shocker.

Matilda downed the rest of her beer, crumpled her empty cup and dropped it. 'This is difficult, isn't it?'

I gripped my beer tighter. 'Is it?'

'Yes,' she said. 'It's like when you're reading a book and you're pretty sure you know what's going to happen next but you're too scared to turn the page in case it doesn't match up to the idea in your head.'

I looked at her and frowned. Was she drunk? She didn't *look* drunk.

Matilda sighed. 'You don't understand, do you?'

'No,' I said – opting for honesty – and I gave her an apologetic shrug.

Matilda twisted round tighter on the step so she was

more or less facing me. 'Don't you think some things are inevitable?'

I felt my frown deepen. Kanye West was singing his 'Gold Digger' song and, at the exact same time, Matilda was wanting to talk about deep and meaningful and *inevitable* things. This party was getting worse and worse. I half wanted my dad to turn up early and rescue me.

Matilda said, 'I believe there are certain things that *are* going to happen because they are *meant* to happen. It's as if the future has already been decided for us and we are like characters in a book.'

'You're drunk,' I said.

'No, I'm not,' said Matilda, and she rolled her eyes annoyed. '*Gottverdammt*, Dylan – I'm trying to tell you something really important.'

I stared back at my beer miserably. Either she was drunk or *I* was. I had absolutely no idea what she was on about. Shaking my head, I said, 'Well, I don't actually believe that anyway. I think we have *tons* of control over our lives – aside from being born and dying, I mean. And if we didn't, we'd all be boring lumps of clay, wouldn't we? Or just like little wooden chess pieces.' I put my horrible beer down on the step below us. '*I'm* not some stupid chess piece. I like listening to rock music and reading poetry and following Bayern Munich football club and being here in Brooklyn and eating as many curried samosas as I can. *That's* what makes me who I am. And none of that has been decided for me by some weird invisible writer. I've decided it all myself.'

Matilda nodded like I'd just made sense. Then she said, 'And what about me?'

This was hard work. Come to think about it, Matilda was *often* hard work. Like that time in the Yu Garden when she'd told me she loved Li. Or that time in Barcelona when she'd embarrassed me in front of her mum. Or too many other times to talk about. Lacing my fingers together, I cracked my knuckles to buy me some time. *Crack. Crack. Crack. Crack.* And after that I sighed and said, 'What *about* you?'

Matilda said, 'Do you like *me*?'

I froze. How was I supposed to answer a question like that? After a delay of maybe several centuries, I opted for honesty again. 'Of course I do,' I said.

Matilda smiled. 'You like me and I like you and here I am on your fifteenth birthday – even though we don't live on the same continent. Don't you think that's almost too perfect? Like something we can't control keeps deliberately bringing us together?'

I bit my lip and nodded. I couldn't take my eyes off her. 'Yeah,' I said, and I was smiling so hard I must have looked like a right goof. 'Your parents wanted a trip to New York and they dragged you along with them. Totally beyond our control.'

Matilda's eyes were looking right into mine. It's like we

were having a staring contest. I don't think I've ever looked at someone for so long without blinking. She said, 'OK, they wanted a trip to New York. But how do you explain the fact that we ever met in the first place?'

'That was just random,' I said.

Matilda frowned. 'And Papa's secondments to Shanghai and Barcelona?'

'Coincidence,' I said. 'Or maybe your family was stalking mine.'

Matilda punched me lightly on my arm. A million megawatts of electricity sparked between us. 'So you think there is no such thing as fate?'

'Nope,' I said.

Matilda bit her lip. 'That's sad,' she said. And by the look on her face, I think she actually *was* sad. 'I felt sure something *really good* was going to happen at this party because it was *meant* to.'

My face started to go hot again. If I'm honest, other parts of my body went hot too. I said, 'What . . . um . . . what did you think was meant to happen?'

Matilda shrugged, rolled her eyes and looked away. 'I don't know. Maybe I was wrong. In which case . . . hey, you know what? It doesn't even matter.'

I panicked then, and a voice in my head said, *Say something, Dylan – do something!* Because it's OK to keep your feelings to yourself for a while but you can't keep them shut up forever. Sometimes in life you have to live a little and risk getting hurt. Call it a cosmic duty, if you like. Collecting together all the courage that I had, I reached out and laid my hand against Matilda's cheek. She turned her head to look at me.

'That thing you thought was inevitable,' I said, 'was it this?' And then I leaned forward and kissed her ever so gently on her lips.

And . . .

BOOM
FIZZ
FIREWORKS

. . . Matilda Sommer was kissing me back.

30

When I found Griff again, he was on his way back up the hill. Hari had gone home and my brother was walking a special sort of walk that anyone would only ever do if they thought they were on their own. He'd looped the strap of his school bag around his forehead and was carrying his bag on his back like a baby in a sling. This freed up his arms so he could pump them backwards and forwards like pistons in order to propel himself up the hill. If I'm honest, he looked a right dick. And if I could have told him that, I definitely would have done. I know he'd have done the same for me. That's what brothers are for.

But when we took the left-hand turn into the hollow in the wood, Griff's arms stopped swinging and he came to a sudden halt. Outside number thirteen Pant-y-Coed was a car. Normally there'd be nothing unusual about that. People parked up on the pavements of Pant-y-Coed all the time. But this car *was* different. Because it had a German licence plate.

'*Gottverdammt*,' I whispered.

'I don't flipping believe it,' whispered Griff.

For a second, we both just stood there, staring in shock at that foreign car. Then Griff tipped his head down, let his bag drop off his head and snatched it up again. Then he walked at high speed to the door.

Inside, the house was full of voices, but when Griff banged the front door shut they all stopped. A heartbeat later, Dee shouted, 'Griff, love, come into the living room, will you?'

Griff raised his hands up to his head and combed his long hair with his fingers. Then he took a deep breath and went further into the house. I followed him.

In the living room, Dee was perched on the edge of an armchair. Almost opposite, Silke and Sven Sommer were sitting next to each other on the sofa. There was no sign of Matilda. I almost collapsed with relief into columns of spiralling dust. I know it sounds weird, but I was *glad* she wasn't there. Seeing her in these circumstances wouldn't have been right. It would have been insubstantial and unreal – sort of like being at a rock festival and watching the whole thing through the screen on my phone.

Griff's face broke into a huge smile. 'I don't believe it,' he said, 'I actually don't believe it.' Turning to Dee he added, 'I kicked the bar on the end of the prom just now.

For luck. It's worked, hasn't it? It's brought Silke and Sven here.'

Dee smiled and pressed her palms together – almost as if she was praying – and Silke and Sven both stood up. 'Look at you, Griff,' said Silke, with tears in her eyes, 'you've grown so tall!' And then she opened up her arms and Griff stepped into them.

I stood just behind Dee and watched my brother being hugged. My own non-existence felt like a dead weight on my back. But then I looked down and something else stirred inside me. It was sympathy for Dee. She looked like she was feeling pretty non-existent herself.

Silke put her hands on my brother's face and said, 'I'm so terribly sorry.'

Griff's eyes flickered downwards.

Dee stood up too. We were all standing in her little living room, and I think that for once everyone else was feeling just about as uncomfortable as I was.

Dee said, 'I tried to phone you, Griff. And I sent texts. I wanted you to know you had visitors.'

Griff took a step away from Silke and freed himself. 'Sorry,' he said. 'I hardly ever look at my phone.' And I remembered then. His phone was still the exact same one he got for his last birthday. And it was always on him – everywhere he went. But it was true – he hardly ever looked at it.

Silke said, 'We would have come sooner, Griff. But we didn't *know*. We got no Christmas card and then I tried to call but the number no longer existed. In the end, I did an Internet search and I . . . I read about what happened.' Her eyes flickered downwards too and she stopped talking.

'So we flew to New York,' said Sven, 'and we spoke to someone at the British Consulate. At first they wouldn't help us or give us any details because we aren't family, but we showed them photos we have of all of us together – right back from when you were a very small child in Munich – and then, *finally*, they told us where we could find you and we came as soon as we could.'

Silke looked up again. Her eyes were red and watery. 'You should have contacted us. We would have come straight away.'

Griff's face had gone very red and he was staring at the carpet. He was probably just trying to stabilise himself. As afternoons go, this one was a total roller coaster.

'I didn't think,' he muttered.

Dee said, 'Can I get anyone some more tea?'

Silke looked at her and smiled gratefully. 'Yes, please.'

Dee ran her hand through her short hair. 'My husband will be home soon. Owen. Will you stay and have a bite to eat with us?'

Sven spoke again. 'Thank you,' he said. 'But we don't want to put you to any trouble.'

'It's no trouble,' said Dee.

'We have dinner included at our hotel,' said Sven. 'In fact, we wondered if Griff would like to join us?'

Griff looked up again and smiled. Then he looked at Dee and looked a bit less happy. 'Um . . . yeah . . . cool,' he said.

Dee put her hand on his back. 'There you are then. That's you sorted. And I dare say it'll beat my spag bol. Now who's for another cuppa?'

Silke and Sven both nodded. Griff shook his head.

When Dee was in the kitchen, Griff said, 'Where's Matilda?'

'She is in Munich with her friend,' said Silke. 'It's not a family outing this time. Sven and I first needed to see that you are OK.'

Griff nodded and gave her a little smile. 'I'm OK.'

Silke took my brother's hand in both of hers and squeezed it. 'And Matilda will be there – when we all get home . . . I mean . . . if . . . if you would like to come back home with us? To Munich, I mean. To be part of our family?'

From the kitchen, there were the sounds of a kettle boiling and Dee rattling cups around. But in the living room, time had stopped passing.

Griff and I stared at Silke in gobsmacked silence.

Then Griff said, 'I . . . er . . .'

Sven stepped forward and touched him on the arm. 'You don't have to say anything now. Think about it. We have a couple of days here in this place before we have to drive back home. But you know . . . it would make us very happy if you came with us. It makes sense. Matilda loves you like a little brother anyway.'

From the kitchen, the kettle had stopped boiling and the cups had stopped rattling. It was as if the whole house was waiting for Griff's reply. I pressed my palms together and waited too.

Griff lifted his other hand and added it to the mid-air hand pile. Then he shook his head sadly – just like Powell had done a few hours earlier. 'Thank you ever so much,' he said. 'It means a lot – it really does.' Letting go of Silke's hand, he rubbed his palm into his eye. 'But I can't do that. Not now. I need to stay here. I really like Dee and Owen and . . . and I've got this friend called Hari . . . She's a girl but she's not my girlfriend or anything . . . she's just really cool and she's teaching me how to play the guitar. And there's Bara Brith the cat . . . She's sort of adopted me as her keeper . . . And there's also this old man called Powell . . . and . . . well . . . I think he'd miss me if I went.' Griff pushed his palm into his other eye and sniffed. 'I think I'd like to learn Welsh too.'

Silke was properly crying now but she nodded and smiled through her tears.

Sven said, 'I don't think we have any Welsh teachers in Munich – you'd be better off here.'

Griff said, 'I'd really like to see Matilda again though.' He smiled a big red blotchy smile. 'Don't tell her I said so – but I think my brother really loved her. Could I come and visit you sometimes?'

297

'Of course,' said Silke. 'Of course.'

'Whenever you like,' said Sven.

Griff smiled and sniffed again. 'Um . . . also, do you mind if I *don't* do the dinner thing tonight? Can we go out tomorrow instead?'

'Of course,' said Silke.

'We'll ask Dee if you can sneak a day off school,' said Sven, 'and then we can have the whole day together – if that's what you'd like.'

Griff nodded. 'I would – definitely.'

Dee came back into the living room carrying a tray with four cups on. She seemed a lot more cheerful than when she'd left. Putting the tray down on the coffee table, she said, 'There's nothing that don't seem better after a cup of Welsh brew.'

When Silke and Sven had gone, Dee said, 'So why didn't you want to go and eat a posh tea with them?'

'I like your spag bol,' said Griff.

Dee looked at him uncertainly for a second. Then she said, 'You're giving me cheek, aren't you? I can't cook for toffee.'

Griff shrugged but then he bit his lip and smiled. 'Neither could my mum. Maybe that's why I like your food.'

Dee's face crumpled into a dimply teary smile. 'Your mam would give you a clip around the ear if she could hear you saying that.'

Griff let out a chuckle. 'I think you'd find that she'd agree with me actually.'

Dee laughed too. Then she said, 'I wasn't listening, love – not really. But did I hear talk of you mitching off school tomorrow?'

Griff bit his lip again. 'Can I? It's almost the end of term. We aren't doing anything important anyway.'

'I suppose one day won't hurt,' said Dee. She laced her fingers together. For a moment I thought she was going to crack her knuckles, but she didn't. Instead she just quietly said, 'I hope you don't change your mind, love.'

It took me a moment to work out what she was on about. I think it took Griff a moment too. But then he said, 'Don't be daft, Dee. I don't want to move to Munich. I want to stay here.'

Dee looked at him. 'Are you sure?'

Griff nodded. 'I am.' He stood up. 'Have I got time to go and listen to some music before tea?'

'You've got a good hour, I reckon,' said Dee. 'O's not back yet, is he?'

Griff picked up his school bag and started walking towards the hall. But just as he got to the door, he paused and looked back at Dee.

She smiled. 'What now?'

Griff chewed his lip and went red. 'Um . . . it's just . . . well . . . I think you and Owen make really top-notch emergency parents.'

For a moment Dee looked utterly metagrobolised. Her face went bright red and she just stared wordlessly at my brother. Then she smiled and said, '*Diolch, Griff, cariad.*' And waving her hand at him like she was waving away a wasp, she half laughed and half cried and said, 'Go away and listen to your music – you're smudging my mascara, you are.'

The Last

Griff's fourteenth birthday was a low-key affair. It's how he wanted it. When Dee had asked him what he'd like to do, my brother had said, 'Nothing much.' And then he'd said, 'Can I just have Hari round? She said she was going to take the guitar lessons to the next level.'

From behind a newspaper, Owen's eyebrows had risen. 'Did she now?'

'Don't be mucky,' said Griff. 'It's not like that. It's a meeting of minds.'

Owen laughed and noisily turned a page. 'A meeting of minds, is it? That's a new one.'

But it meant that Griff's birthday – which had been lurking on the horizon like storm clouds – ended up being easy. Dee and Owen gave him a guitar and I saw the sun come out on his face. Two parcels arrived with foreign postmarks on as well. There was a Bayern Munich football top from Matilda and Silke and Sven, and a very special delivery of a rare 1961 Aretha Franklin original record from Blessing, Marlon and Pudders. Blessing must have liked my brother a lot.

And then there was the gift from Hari. Like Blessing's package, it was LP-shaped. It was wrapped in brown parcel paper with hand-drawn plectrums all over it.

'This better be Lynx shower gel,' said Griff when we were up in his bedroom – just him, Hari, the cat and me.

'Got it in one, Griffindor,' said Hari.

When the paper came off, Griff beamed. 'Oh my God,' he said. 'Thank you *so* much!'

Hari shrugged and tried to look cool, but anyone could see she was beaming too. 'It *is* the right one, isn't it?'

'It's exactly the right one,' said Griff. 'The Beach Boys *20/20*. How did you get Lew to sell it?' He lowered the record and suddenly looked worried. 'Please don't say you let him touch your cheekbones.'

'*Shuddup!*' said Hari, appalled. 'Lew had nothing to do with it. I found a copy online. The sleeve is a bit scruffy but the record's all right.'

Griff slid the big circle of black vinyl out of its cardboard sleeve and put it carefully on the turntable of his ancient stereo. Then he flicked a switch on the wall, pressed a few buttons on the retro music machine and put the needle down on the record. There was a loud crackle and a fuzzy hiss and then the sweet sound of the Beach

Boys filled the bedroom. Even Bara Brith purred and seemed pleased.

Griff swallowed hard. 'It's weird,' he said. 'I should probably hate this record because when I first heard it I was mostly wishing I was dead. But . . . I dunno . . . listening to this is one of those little tiny things that make me want to be alive.' He looked at Hari anxiously. 'Does that even make sense?'

Hari nodded and unzipped her guitar case. 'Totally. I can't imagine the world without decent tunes in it.' Her eyes flicked over to the wall. 'You've put a new picture up,' she said.

Griff and I turned to look. Alongside the Beatles on their stripy crosswalk and Kurt Cobain puffing on his roll-up and Beyoncé in her foxy leotard and Dylan Thomas in his tragic tank top, there was a new picture. I leaned in and looked closer. It was one of my whole family. Me and Griff and Mum and Dad. We were standing at the Top of the Rock and smiling, high above New York City.

Griff folded his arms so tightly that he looked like he was giving himself a hug. 'That's them,' he said to Hari. 'It's from quite a few years ago, but I love that picture. We were on top of the Rockefeller Center and me and Dyl nearly puked because Mum and Dad had a snog.' A faraway fuzziness softened his eyes. 'Well, it wasn't *actually* a snog – he just kissed her. But I'm glad he did that now.'

Hari tickled Bara Brith's head. Then she picked up her

guitar and held it ready to play. 'So are we gonna take this guitar playing to the next level or what?'

Griff's eyes cleared. Picking up his own guitar, he said, 'At least I don't have to borrow yours any more, Harold.'

'We're both pleased about that,' said Hari. 'You can snap your own strings now.' Wrapping her hand around the neck of the guitar, she picked out a chord and began strumming in time with the Beach Boys. 'So today,' she said, 'we're doing *bar* chords. You're gonna need all your fingers, Griffindor.' And to prove the point, she contorted one hand into the most uncomfortable shape ever to show him exactly how it was done.

Griff tried to copy her. After a few failed attempts to get all his fingers in all the right places, he frowned and said, 'Can't we just stick with the chords we know?'

Hari shook her head. 'Not unless you want to play "Wonderwall" forever. Or "Michael Row the Boat Ashore".'

Griff frowned deeper and tried again. After a moment or so he looked up and said, 'So what songs can we play with these dumb bar chords?'

Hari shrugged. 'Anything you like. I was thinking of starting with "Smells Like Teen Spirit".'

Time stopped.

But then it found its rhythm again.

Griff pulled a face. 'I'm not mad keen on that one,' he said. 'But do you know "Heart-shaped Box" or "About a Girl"?'

And suddenly – at that exact second – I couldn't bear to be there any longer. It didn't feel right. It didn't feel decent. It was like I was muscling in on an ordinary special moment. So, reaching out, I put my hand on my brother's arm to let him know I was finally going.

Griff's fingers went still on his guitar and his head turned slightly to one side. To me.

'As long as I'm in there,' I said, gently touching Griff's forehead, 'I'm always, always here. That's how close I am. It's not like getting on the train and going to Shrewsbury or Birmingham or anything. You only have to think about me to cover the distance.'

And I know he heard me because he flashed a sudden little grin at Hari and said, 'I'm thinking about Dyl. I'm thinking about how impressed he'd be that I'm actually learning to play Nirvana songs on the guitar.'

Hari looked serious for a second, but then her face broke out into a big wide smile and soon they were both just sitting there – her and Griff – with these huge happy grins on their faces. And I was smiling too because life is beautiful sometimes.

But it was time to go. My mum and dad were waiting for me and I wanted to leave this world and wait for Matilda in the next one. And I wanted to wait for her for years and years and years and not a single moment less. I looked back one last time at Griff. It seemed like he was finally winning with that bar chord. And as I walked towards the light, a new song began to play. It was that one by the Beach Boys, 'The Nearest Faraway Place'. It sounded like the exit music to a film. Sad and sweet and hopeful ever after.

Griff's Playlist For Powell

1. Gold Digger - Kanye West
2. It's Like That — Run DMC Vs Jason Nevins
3. Song 2 — Blur
4. Star Sign - Teenage Fanclub
5. Whirring — The Joy Formidable *
6. I Say a Little Prayer - Aretha Franklin
7. American Boy - Estelle
8. Stutter - Elastica
9. Union City Blue - Blondie
10. About a Girl — Nirvana
11. Empire State of Mind - Alicia Keys
12. Catch the Sun - Doves
13. God! Show Me Magic - Super Furry Animals *
14. When Doves Cry - Prince
15. Indie Cindy — Pixies
16. Halo - Beyoncé
17. Slide Away - Oasis
18. Cannonball - The Breeders
19. Here Comes the Sun - The Beatles
20. The Nearest Faraway Place - The Beach Boys.

* These ones are Welsh.

Acknowledgements

The Nearest Faraway Place would not be the book it is without the support I've received from a number of very sparky people. First of all, there is my agent, Tim Bates – once again, he took my words and found them a home and offered me a truckload of encouragement along the way. Then there is Emma Matthewson, my editor at Hot Key Books. An idea from Emma is an idea worth running with and I'm lucky to have had her input in this story and in *Sophie Someone* too. Enormous thanks must also go to Talya Baker, who really helped to make Dylan's voice sparkle, and to Alexandra Allden who designed the seriously lovely cover; and thanks, too, to *all* the team at Hot Key Books. I'm also hugely appreciative of – and flattered by – the kind words of Kerstin at Koenigskinder and Christine at Gallimard who read a draft copy of *TNFP* and snapped it up for German and French audiences. *Danke* and *merci*!

And then there is Gwen Davies in Aberystwyth. Gwen has a cat called Bara Brith who walked straight into the pages of this novel. Five minutes spent in Gwen's company is enough to remind me that working with words has made me some amazing friends. And also in Wales, there is my dear old pal Lynda Jones, who I've known almost forever. We regularly chat on the phone and Lynda effortlessly drops in comments about Einstein and $E = mc^2$ and the theory of relativity and says stuff like 'all that energy has to go somewhere' – and she makes me just . . . well . . . *think*!

And, crucially, there is Graham Tomlinson – who married me. He is lovely and patient and supportive and I couldn't do without him. Also, not very long ago, he waved a Beach Boys CD in my face and said, 'There's a track on here called "The Nearest Faraway Place". I think that's the idea you are trying to capture.' ♥

And that reminds me – The Beach Boys, Nirvana, Aretha Franklin, Beyoncé and the poet Dylan Thomas . . . I love you all. As I love YOU, sweet reader. For giving me your support by reading this book.

Thanks.

Want to read
NEW BOOKS
before anyone else?

Like getting
FREE BOOKS?

Enjoy sharing your
OPINIONS?

Discover

**READERS
FIRST**

Read. Love. Share.

Get your first free book just by signing up at
readersfirst.co.uk

HOT KEY BOOKS

Thank you for choosing a Hot Key book.

If you want to know more about our authors
and what we publish, you can find us online.

You can start at our website

www.hotkeybooks.com

And you can also find us on:

We hope to see you soon!